"You can't be mine," Aristos rasped, his gaze tracking her. "You w⬛⬛⬛⬛ list again? I d⬛⬛⬛ ⬛⬛ Alex. My aff⬛⬛ ⬛⬛ ⬛ commitmen⬛ ⬛⬛ ⬛⬛ature. You are off-limits."

"What if I did...want that, I mean."

His gaze narrowed. "You are a princess. Third-in-line to the throne, in case you'd forgotten. Who I'm supposed to be protecting."

"There's no threat here," she derided. "The only thing you're protecting me from is you."

"Damn right."

She took a deep breath. Maybe the deepest she'd ever taken. Lifted her chin. "What you said last night..."

He gave her a suspicious look. "Which part would that be?"

"The *incendiary* part. I would...like that."

His eyes widened. He set his glass down on the railing. "Are you trying to destroy my head?"

She shook her head. "I'm suggesting, as you said, we do what we both want to do. Nobody needs to know."

A long moment passed. "Just so we're clear," he ventured in a silky voice, "you're suggesting we have an affair? Confined to this island?"

"Yes."

Jennifer Hayward invites you into a world of...

Kingdoms & Crowns

Young royals in reckless pursuit of passion!

When a centuries-old battle between the Kingdoms of Akathinia and Carnelia is reignited, the nation's young royals find themselves on the brink of war. But their kingdoms aren't the only thing at stake...

Soon these young monarchs are facing an unexpected royal baby, the appearance of a lost princess and an alliance with the enemy.

Can love conquer all? Find out in:

King Nikandros & Sofia Ramirez's story

Carrying the King's Pride

March 2016

Princess Aleksandra & Aristos Nicolades's story

Claiming the Royal Innocent

May 2016

And look for

King Kostas & Princess Stella's story

Coming soon!

Jennifer Hayward

CLAIMING THE ROYAL INNOCENT

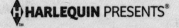

Recycling programs
for this product may
not exist in your area.

ISBN-13: 978-0-373-13436-6

Claiming the Royal Innocent

First North American Publication 2016

Printed in U.S.A.

www.Harlequin.com

Jennifer Hayward has been a fan of romance since filching her sister's novels to escape her teenage angst. Her career in journalism and PR—including years of working alongside powerful, charismatic CEOs and traveling the world—has provided her with perfect fodder for the fast-paced, sexy stories she likes to write, always with a touch of humor. A native of Canada's East Coast, Jennifer lives in Toronto with her Viking husband and young Viking-in-training.

Visit the Author Profile page
at Harlequin.com for more titles.

This one is for my brother, Andrew, and his unfailing belief in me in following my dream. It's true—dreams aren't too expensive to keep! xx

CHAPTER ONE

"THE COUNT AND Countess of Agiero."

A soldier in ceremonial uniform announced the exquisitely dressed couple queued in front of Aleksandra Dimitriou in the foyer of the Akathinian royal palace ballroom, his booming voice with its perfect elocution sending her heart plunging to the marble floor. She had hoped arriving late for Princess Stella's twenty-fifth birthday party would mean the introductions would have been long concluded.

But then again, what did she know? She had never attended a high society party before, let alone an official royal function. The blue silk gown she wore was rented from one of those designer dress services that mailed the couture creation to you in exchange for an exorbitant amount of money, her shoes were those of her fashionable friend Kira, her jewelry unearthed in a knockoff boutique in the city. In fact, not even the invitation belonged to her. She had *stolen* it with the intent of slipping in unnoticed.

The furor in her head, gathering momentum by the minute, suggested her ploy was about to be revealed to the hundreds of people gathered to celebrate the princess's birthday. Not to mention the dozens of paparazzi who stood poised like a flock of vultures behind the stanchioned-off red carpet waiting for a money shot.

Her palms went sweaty. A shot of *her* in handcuffs, a *royal intruder* caught red-handed during a time of high security for the country, would be great fodder for them. She could just see the residents of her small, sleepy coastal village waking up to her face splashed across the front page of the daily newspaper. Picture them doing a double take, their bemusement quickly turning to horror…

Her heart pounded madly against her ribs. There was no way she was going to pull this off. She should turn around and go back to Stygos and forget she'd ever had this stupid, foolish need to know a piece of herself. To right a wrong that had long since been undoable.

But it was too late to back out now. The palace official was reaching for her blue and gold-embossed invitation, an expectant smile on his face. She handed it to him with frozen fingers. He checked his list. Frowned. Ran his finger over the names again, then looked up at her. "*Lypamai, despoinis*, but your name doesn't seem to be on the list."

Alex swallowed hard. Summoned composure from a place deep inside her she hadn't even known existed. "I originally had to decline the invitation," she said smoothly. "When I found out I would be in the country, I sent another note accepting."

He procured another list, scanned it, consulted someone by radio, then nodded. "*Kala.* It's fine. You're on the original list." He passed the invitation to the soldier with the booming voice and nodded for her to proceed. "Enjoy your evening."

She pinned a smile on her lips, picked up the hem of her gown and moved toward the entrance to the ballroom.

"*Kara Nicholson,*" the soldier announced, his deep baritone seeming to hang on the air forever. Alex's step faltered, a thin layer of perspiration breaking out on her brow as she waited for someone to point out that she was *not* Kara Nicholson. That she was a *fraud.*

The din of the crowd remained unchanged. The soldier gave her a curious look. Exhaling the breath she'd been holding, she propelled herself forward on legs that shook so badly it was hard to put one foot in front of the other.

The powder room was her first priority. There, she restored her outward composure with her makeup compact. Inner composure, however, was somewhat more elusive.

That she and Kara, the American heiress who'd stayed in her family's tourist hotel a few weeks ago, were both slim with dark hair and blue eyes had just saved her from certain disaster. It was Kara's discarded invitation she'd picked out of the trash can to gain admittance to the party. Kara's identity she'd assumed. But resembling the beautiful socialite and being in any way prepared to do what she'd come here to do, to mingle with the exclusive crowd Kara frequented, were two entirely different things.

You just have to fake it long enough to get this done. Jaw set, shoulders back, she made her way into the elegantly clad crowd that filled the magnificent sweeping ballroom, champagne flutes in their hands. The upper echelons of Akathinian society were in attendance to celebrate the princess's birthday—assorted celebrities and a smattering of royalty from across Europe. The kind of people she checked into her hotel for a quiet, idyllic week where they wouldn't be bothered, the best view in all of Akathinia offered from their seaside window. Not those she socialized with.

She plucked a glass of champagne off a waiter's tray and moved deeper into the thick crowd, searching for a spot to locate her target. Taking a long sip of the delicious, clearly outrageously expensive bubbly, she swallowed, the champagne fizzling its way down to her stomach, where it spread a slow warmth through her. Exactly what she needed.

Securing a quiet corner from which she could survey the room, she tucked herself against a pillar and drank in her spectacular surroundings. Lit in the same blue and gold tones as the invitation, the richly appointed ballroom was a feast for the eye. The Akathinian royal crest was projected onto black marble floors, which looked as if they were threaded through with real gold vein. Massive antique chandeliers glittered from the ceiling, serving as a brilliant counterpoint for the dark accents in the room, while precious, larger-than-life paintings adorned walls that soared to impressive thirty-foot heights.

Her head spun at the opulence of it all. None of it seemed real. But then again, nothing *had* seemed real since her mother, a former lady-in-waiting to the elder Queen Amara, had broken a twenty-five-year silence with a bombshell that had blown her life apart.

Her father had not been an Akathinian businessman who had died before her birth. He was King Gregorios, the former monarch of this country, with whom her mother had carried out an extended affair before the queen discovered her betrayal and fired her.

Her hand trembled as she downed another swallow of champagne. That her mother, whom she'd considered above reproach, whose strength and courage symbolized everything that was good in the world, had indulged in a dangerous, illicit affair with the king, a married man, then manufactured a series of elaborate stories to paint a rosy view of her childhood, for whatever altruistic reasons she cared to offer, seemed inconceivable. *Unimaginable.*

And yet it was the truth. She had a father she'd never known. The siblings she'd longed for as a child, all of whom would have been lost to her if her mother hadn't broken down and told her the truth.

A bright burst of laughter drew her gaze. Princess Stella, *her half sister*, clad in a dazzling silver gown, held court in the center of the room, a handful of handsome men arranged around her, vying for her attention. She looked every inch the Grecian goddess with her slim figure and sleek blond hair caught up in an elaborate twist. Every inch a princess.

How different would her life have been had her mother told her the truth? Would she have become a princess, glittering alongside her sophisticated elder sister? Would she never have known her quiet, idyllic life in Stygos?

A fist tightened in her chest. How her half siblings would receive her was yet to be determined. Her priority, however, was her father's ill health, which had made tonight's subterfuge necessary. A heart attack had sent King Gregorios back to the hospital, his absence tonight marked. She needed to meet him before he died. It was the only thing that *had* been clear in the confusion of the past few months.

She scanned the room, locating the young, strikingly handsome King Nikandros mingling with a group of guests, his wife, Sofía, by his side. *Her brother.*

Nikandros had ascended to the throne after his father's initial heart attack during a difficult time for Akathinia, with its aggressive sister island Carnelia threatening to annex Akathinia back into the Catharian island group to which it had once belonged. Many feared the seventy-year-old Carnelian King Idas might finally have lost his mind, his recent mobilization of the Carnelian military suggesting a war might be on its way.

Thus the reason she had chosen tonight as her avenue to speak to the king. Securing an audience with him under any other circumstances would have been nearly impossible given the security that surrounded him and the demands on his time.

So tonight it was. She set her flute down on a waiter's tray with a determined *clink* of crystal. Took another. The expensive vintage was boosting her confidence by the minute, easing the tightness in her chest as it filled her with its insidious warmth. After this glass, she'd work up the courage to do what she needed to do. To rock the royal family with a scandal at a time when it needed it the least.

* * *

Aristos Nicolades leaned against a column in the packed ballroom, watching the stunning brunette in the sexy blue gown toss back her second glass of champagne with a speed that suggested she needed courage of some sort.

For what? he wondered idly, studying the play of shimmering light as it highlighted every dip and curve of her petite, shapely figure. Considering she'd lied about who she was to gain admittance to the party, he'd thought it best to keep an eye on her.

He'd been behind her in the lineup to the ballroom, his flight from the United States delayed, making him almost an hour late for the party. His every desire had been to skip the event, go home, take a long, hot shower and sleep after a grueling week abroad. But considering the king had finally granted him a license to build the jewel in his crown, a new casino on the sparkling, glitterati-strewn Mediterranean island of Akathinia, giving the occasion a miss had not been an option.

Bemused when the blue-gowned angel had swanned up to the doors of the ballroom and announced herself as Kara Nicholson, he thought he'd been hallucinating after almost thirty-six hours without sleep. The Kara Nicholson he'd divested of her clothes before he'd taken her in a long, hot encounter in Vegas six months ago, the Kara Nicholson known to travel in Stella's circles, was *not* the brunette standing in front of him.

With her near-angelic look—all big blue eyes and long, satiny dark hair—she hardly seemed the type to be one of Carnelia's spies or, God forbid, worse. But nothing could be discounted in this time of tension—spies had been pinpointed; separatist factions had emerged—and considering that a satellite company of his was in charge of security tonight, he wasn't taking any chances.

He studied the nerves the beautiful brunette was clearly

fighting despite her attempt at outward composure. She had come alone, hadn't attempted to talk to anyone, clearly knew no one here. The only person she had shown an interest in, other than the fleeting glances she'd been sending his way as an immediate attraction had sparked between them, had been the king. She had been inordinately interested in his whereabouts ever since she'd arrived.

It was possible she was simply one of those women who couldn't seem to accept that King Nikandros was happily married. There were enough of them around. Perhaps a jilted ex-lover? It would fit with the lost look she had at the moment…the inherent aura of vulnerability that surrounded her.

She sensed his perusal. Turned her chin to meet his gaze. The confusion, the anxiety in her beautiful blue eyes, stoked his curiosity higher. Confusion that quickly morphed into the unmistakable interest he'd seen there before. He held her gaze. Sustained the connection. Electricity arced between them, a rosy pink staining her cheeks.

Dipping her chin, she broke the contact first in one of those shy gestures that didn't seem to fit with the sexy image. A plus B plus C wasn't adding up.

His curiosity got the better of him. Downing his last swallow of scotch, he set the glass on a table and headed toward her. He'd played games he'd enjoyed far less than the one he was playing now. *This* could prove highly enjoyable.

Thee mou. He was headed over here.

Alex swallowed hard, wondering what on earth she was doing. She was here to talk to her father, to know him before he died, not flirt with the most strikingly good-looking male she'd ever seen, in a tuxedo or out of one. Yet *he* had been staring at her, making no effort to hide his interest. Difficult to ignore, particularly since every time she worked up the courage to speak to King Nikandros, he had moved on to another group.

Meanwhile, doubts were piling up about whether it had been an extremely bad idea to choose this party as the venue for her mission as the king glittered as an untouchable force. Would her father even want to see her? Would he even care she existed? Would he toss her out without acknowledging her?

Her ruminations were interrupted by the scent of expensive aftershave, followed by the man who wore it. He was tall, well over six feet, his height backed up by the lean, hard-packed muscle that covered every inch of him. With his dark-as-sin eyes and designer stubble, he made every other man in the room look effeminate in comparison.

Undeniably intimidating. Insanely attractive.

"I was standing over there wondering why a beautiful woman finds herself alone throwing back champagne like water." The rich, velvety undertone to his voice stoked every nerve ending to full attention. "Rather than allow my imagination to conjure up all sorts of creative possibilities, I thought I would simply come over and ask."

Her eyes slid to her empty glass. "It's only my second."

"In rapid succession." He swept his dark gaze over her in a perusal that scorched her skin. "To provide courage perhaps?"

She tossed her hair over her shoulders. "Why would I need courage?"

His eyes glittered with amusement. "You tell me. You are here alone. Perhaps that makes you feel uncomfortable?"

Very. She lifted a shoulder in what she hoped was a nonchalant gesture. "I have business to attend to. It's not so much a social occasion for me."

"Business at a birthday party? How distasteful."

"A personal matter."

He inclined his head. "Perhaps you could combine your

personal matter with a little…*pleasure.* I find myself at loose ends."

She suspected this man hadn't spent one second of his life at loose ends, but his sexy drawl had the intended effect, tangling her up inside.

"You look quite comfortable at loose ends."

"I prefer to find a…*diversion.* And you," he said, holding her gaze, "are the most beautiful woman in the room."

Her stomach flip-flopped, a wave of betraying heat rising from her chest to fill her cheeks. "Hardly true. The princess is hosting, after all."

"She has a layer of ice that surrounds her. You do not."

Alex swallowed past the sudden dryness in her throat, finding herself unable to pull her gaze away from his smoky, sexy one. "I'm afraid I'm not available as a diversion."

"Because you are here for someone else?"

"Because I really must see who I need to see, then go."

"One dance." He held out a lean-fingered, bronzed hand. "Then you can get on with your business."

He made it seem rude, *impolite* to refuse. Over his shoulder, she could see the king and queen still immersed in conversation. Perhaps it *would* be better to say yes to a dance rather than stand around at loose ends looking painfully out of place as she clearly had been.

"All right," she said, placing her palm in his much larger one. "I would love to."

He wrapped his fingers around hers. "Aristos," he drawled. "And you are…?"

Her brain froze, her clear thinking not aided by the two glasses of champagne she'd consumed. "Kara," she said after a pause. Better to continue the facade.

Not that it was easy to keep anything straight in her head with the energy that pulsed between them, moving from his fingers through her body until she was buzzing with the intensity of it.

His tall, impressive physique parted the crowds easily as he led her toward the dance floor, where a live band was playing a slow, sexy jazz number.

Aristos laced his fingers through hers, slid his arm around her waist and pulled her into a close hold that had her pulse racing. His smooth, skillful steps as he directed her around the packed space surprised her for such a solidly built male.

"So," he said, leveling his gaze on her face, "how do you know the princess?"

Her stomach seized. *A natural question*, she told herself. *Relax.*

"We're friends," she said, repeating what Kara had told her. "We're on a few of the same charitable boards."

He inclined his head. "And what do you do when you aren't tending to these…*charitable endeavors*?"

She blinked. Thought furiously. But a few scattered conversations with Kara hadn't provided that depth of information. "Mostly that," she murmured awkwardly. "My father has a large philanthropic portfolio. He needs the help."

"And where is home?"

"Texas," she said faintly, as if that would make up for her lack of a drawl.

"Funny, you don't *sound* like a Southerner."

Her mouth went even drier. *Diavole*, but this had been a bad idea. "I think I've lost my accent," she prevaricated. "I travel so much I've become somewhat…international."

His mouth twisted. "I get that one hundred percent. It's the same with me." His hand tightened around hers as he spun her in a smooth circle. "Texas is a big state. Which part?"

She had no idea. "Dallas," she said, guessing.

"The home of J.R. Ewing…"

She smiled a tight smile. "The very same. And you?"

she asked, attempting to regain control of the conversation. "How do you know Stella?"

"I'm a business partner of the king."

Oh, no. Not good. Swallowing her panic, she lifted her gaze to his. "What business would that be?"

"Hotels and casinos. A bit of this, a bit of that."

She thought that fit perfectly with his dark, edgy vibe. "That must be a very...*interesting* world."

His mouth quirked. "You don't sound so sure about that."

She lifted a shoulder. "I'm not a gambler. It seems to me you prey on the vulnerable. Take unsuspecting people's money."

"Those who walk into a casino do so of their own volition."

"Yes," she agreed, "but do they always know their limits?"

"They should. I find there is an epidemic of late of people who have no sense of personal responsibility. We are all responsible for our own actions."

Yes, she agreed silently, hysteria biting at the edges of her composure. That concept was top of mind at the moment.

"Perhaps true," she conceded. "Although I'm not sure it's a fair comparison. I'm an idealist. I think we all need to be looking out for the greater good."

"A dying breed," he said softly, his dark gaze resting on her face. "Idealists..."

He left it at that. She shut up before she said something she shouldn't. She should have protested when he tugged her closer so his tall, muscular body brushed against hers, his chin resting atop her head. But when there was no talking involved, there was no danger in exposing herself.

She couldn't resist allowing herself to melt into all that strength, just for a moment, of course, until the dance was over. It felt hedonistically good, frankly exciting to be in his arms, and when would she ever have another chance to meet a man like him? Stunning-looking members of the opposite sex were a precious commodity in Stygos. She'd known all of them since childhood.

The plaintive, haunting notes of the saxophone were beautiful. The champagne had kicked in full force now, leaving in its wake a heady buzzing feeling that instilled a confidence in her she hadn't had before. It made the dangerous attraction she felt toward the man holding her even more powerful. Made her even more aware of the strong column of his thighs as they pressed against her, driving home how powerfully built he was. How the spicy scent of his cologne mixed with the heady male musk of him was doing crazy things to her insides...

The warmth of his hand splayed at her waist burned her skin like a brand through the thin silk of her dress. It made her wonder what it would be like to be touched by him. *Truly* touched by him.

Her champagne-clouded brain was floating in a sea of pheromones when the song came to an end. She moved to extract her fingers from his, but he tightened his hold. "One more."

She should have ended it right there. But it was far too tempting to say yes. A glance over his shoulder revealed the king still deep in conversation. How harmful was one more dance?

He pulled her closer, their bodies perfectly aligning as they moved to the sultry notes of the song. It was an inappropriate hold, she knew, the heat of him moving through her like the most potent of caresses, his hand drifting lower to lie against the small of her back. But her sensible side seemed to have deserted her. He was the dark, mysterious hero of her favorite novels come to life, with a dangerous, presumptive twist that was impossible to resist.

A couple more minutes and she'd go.

She thought maybe a third song had come and gone when she finally pulled her head from where it was nestled under his chin and realized they had gradually worked their way from the couples dancing along the edge of the ballroom to the shadows of the small terrace that led off it.

She looked up into the mesmerizing heat of his black gaze, suddenly aware of exactly where this was going. "I told you I'm not interested in being a diversion," she reminded him a little too breathlessly.

"No?" he said derisively, bending his head toward her. "Your signals are saying the contrary." Sliding his fingers around her jaw, he captured her lips in a kiss unlike any she'd had before. Cajoling and demanding her acquiescence all at the same time, it was sensual, playful and masterful, enticing her to respond to his seductive expertise.

Her lips clung to his, helpless to resist his slow, intoxicating kisses. She swayed closer to him, her hand settling on his waist. He drew her into his warmth, the proximity of their bodies sending a shiver through her.

He lifted his lips from hers, their breath mingling. "Open your mouth, angel."

She hadn't been aware she was denying him anything. Obeying his command, she allowed his firm, beautiful mouth to part hers in a hot, languorous exploration she felt right down to her toes.

Her sigh split the air. He moved his hands down to her hips and shaped her buttocks, drawing her even closer to him until their bodies were molded together without a centimeter between them. She could feel the hard heat of him burning against the juncture of her thighs, as impressive as the rest of him. It made her knees weak.

"Aristos," she gasped, pulling her mouth from his. "Stop."

Satisfaction laced his gaze as she stared up at him, the supreme control she found there snapping her out of her haze. She put a palm against his chest to put some distance between them, but the hand he held at the small of her back kept her where she was. He slid it down over her buttock to wrap around her thigh.

"What *are* you doing?" she demanded, pushing harder against the rock-solid wall of his chest to no avail.

"Checking for weapons."

"Weapons?" Her brain struggled to compute. "Why would I be carrying weapons?"

He ran his palm over her other buttock and down the back of her thigh in a leisurely exploration that brought a heated wave to her cheeks. "Maybe you should tell me, *Kara.*"

The edge to his voice made the hairs on the back of her neck stand up. *He knows. Had known all this time.*

She pushed a hand against his chest and this time he released her, setting her away from him. She bit down into her lip. *Hard.* "You know I'm not Kara."

He raked his gaze over her face. "Correct, angel. So maybe you'd care to tell me what you're doing here. And why you impersonated Kara Nicholson to get in."

A buzzing sound filled her ears. "How did you know?"

"Well, let's see… Your accent, for starters. Second, Kara is from *Houston*, not Dallas. And finally, I happen to know Kara. *Intimately.* And *you* are not her."

Thee mou. She closed her eyes, cheeks flaming. He and Kara Nicholson were lovers. How could she have ever thought she'd get away with this?

She opened her eyes. "You were behind me in line. Why didn't you call me out then?"

"I wanted to see what your intentions were."

"What did you *think* I was doing?"

"We have a country trying to draw us into a war, in case you hadn't noticed."

Disbelief sank through her. "You think I'm a spy? An *assassin?*"

"I think when anyone enters an official royal engagement under false pretenses, it needs to be investigated."

"So you thought you'd appoint yourself investigator? *Maul me* while you're at it? Make a game of it?"

"I wouldn't call it mauling. You were as into that as I was. And as for my *interest* in you, it's my security team the palace is using tonight. A side business of mine, angel, along with my *big, bad* casinos. I wasn't about to set you loose with the king in the room."

She clenched her hands at her sides, her gaze fixed on his. "You are going to regret this."

An amused glimmer filled his eyes. "Really? Do tell. My guess from the way you've been eyeing the king is that you're an ex-lover. A jilted one, perhaps... You don't seem—how should I put it?—*off your rocker*, so I'm assuming you've come with some misguided belief he'll take a lover. I hate to break it to you, but he's madly in love with his wife. It isn't going to happen."

A jilted lover? She gaped at him. "Are you out of your mind?"

He lifted a shoulder. "I've seen the women who throw themselves at the king. They crash parties to meet him. They go to ridiculous lengths to get his attention. So even though you," he said, stripping the clothes from her with a look that singed her skin, "are undoubtedly every man's type, *this* was a wasted escapade."

Fury swelled up inside her. "I came tonight because I need to speak to the king about a personal matter. Just like I said earlier."

"Why do it under false pretenses?"

"It's complicated."

"Complicated *how*?"

"That's my business."

"I'm afraid it's mine if you don't want me to have you handcuffed and hauled out of here right now."

"You wouldn't."

"Try me."

Her heart surged painfully against her chest. Pressing her hands to her face, she paced to the other side of the terrace. "I can't tell you why. I admit my methods for getting here were unconventional, but they were necessary given the security surrounding the king. I would never have gotten an audience."

"That security is in place for a good reason."

"Yes," she said, turning around. "It is." She took a deep breath. Fixed him with an imploring look. "I promise you it's imperative I speak to the king. In fact, if you would just take me to him right now, I would highly appreciate it."

"Not happening until you tell me who you are and what your business is."

"I can't."

"Kala." He spun on his heel and stalked toward the door.

"Aristos, stop."

He turned around. "No one knows this," she said. "You can't say anything to anyone."

"Spit it out," he growled.

She lifted her chin. "My name is Aleksandra Dimitriou. The king is my half brother."

CHAPTER TWO

ARISTOS'S MOUTH WENT SLACK. *Nikandros's half sister.* He couldn't have heard her correctly.

"Can you please," he said deliberately, "repeat that?"

Aleksandra, *if that was even her right name*, rubbed a hand against her temple. "My mother, Melaina, was Queen Amara's lady-in-waiting. She had an affair with King Gregorios during her tenure at the palace. The queen knew about her husband's indiscretions, but when she discovered the affair with my mother, it was one step too far. She fired her. No one knew my mother was pregnant. She went home to her village and raised me by herself."

He blinked. "Why keep it a secret? By Akathinian law, you would have been a royal."

"My mother knew I would be taken away from her if anyone found out. She didn't want that life for me. She told everyone, including me, that my father was an Akathinian businessman she'd met while she worked at the palace who was killed in a car accident before I was born. It wasn't until the king had his heart attack that I learned the truth."

Thee mou. His head spun. The queen's lady-in-waiting. *The ultimate betrayal.*

It was well-known that King Gregorios had indulged in countless affairs. But a child kept secret this long? Born to the queen's most trusted aide? If true, it was a scandal that would put all before it to shame.

He scrutinized the woman in front of him. Was she telling the truth? Her skin was pale beneath her olive-toned complexion, the vulnerability that emanated from her a quality he didn't think could be manufactured. Nor did he think she was a threat to anyone. She was not a practiced liar, that was clear. But he had learned long ago never to trust first impressions. Particularly when it came to a woman—the most deceptive creature on the face of the earth. One who wanted an audience with the king.

It hit him then, that same feeling of familiarity he'd experienced from the first moment he'd seen her. *Those eyes...* That particular shade of blue belonged to only one bloodline he knew. They were Constantinides blue. It was like looking at Nikandros and Stella.

His blood ran cold. She was telling the truth.

Aleksandra pressed her lips together. "I told you you were going to regret doing *that*."

He closed his eyes. For once in his life, he did. He and the king had just gotten their relationship on a solid footing after an adversarial start. *This* he didn't need.

"Just because you have the Constantinides eyes, as rare as they are, doesn't mean your story is true," he said roughly. "It will need to be verified, as I'm sure you will appreciate. You can understand my suspicions."

Her eyes flashed. "Your suspicions, yes, but not your tactics."

"Like I said, it took two to make *that* kiss."

That shut her up. He paced to the edge of the terrace, his brain working furiously. They were smack in the middle of a royal function with every paparazzo camera, gossip and royal watcher in the country in their midst. This could not get out before it was verified and the ramifications considered. But that was the king's job—not his.

He closed the distance between them. "What were your intentions coming here tonight? What do you want from the king?"

"I want to see my father. Talk to him. That's all."

He studied her for a long moment. Cursed under his breath and pulled his mobile phone from the inside pocket of his jacket. A phone call to the man in charge of security brought a detail in a dark suit out to the terrace.

"This is how this is going to go," he said to Aleksandra. "*You* are going to stay here with him. You do not move from here, you do not talk to anyone and if you do, he will restrain you. Understood?"

Her eyes widened, skin paling. "Yes."

She looked as if a good gust of wind might blow her over. Intensely vulnerable. His heart contracted despite his effort to stay distanced from the explosive situation unfolding in front of him. It had taken an immense amount of courage for her to come here and do what she'd done. He could only imagine how terrified she felt.

Closing the gap between them, he slid his fingers under her chin and brought her gaze up to his. "The king is a good man. You have nothing to fear."

He, on the other hand, did, if she spilled what had just happened to Nikandros.

Alex's heart thudded painfully beneath her ribs as her rather ominous-looking security detail nodded at her to precede him into the room. She stepped inside the palace library, its elegant chandeliers and wall sconces illuminating shelf upon shelf of precious volumes.

With her voracious passion for literature, the shelves might have stolen her attention had it not been fixed on the man who stood at the far end of the room looking out the windows, hands buried in his pockets.

She stood there, fingers biting into her tiny silk clutch as the king turned around and studied her, his expression intent. His eyes widened imperceptibly, then that perfectly controlled countenance that made him vastly intimidating resumed its tenure.

He turned to Aristos. *"Efharisto."*

Aristos nodded and headed for the door. She fought the crazy urge to beg him to stay—he who had threatened to put her in handcuffs and have her tossed out—but after a long glance at her that seemed to say *keep your head up, you can do this*, he left, the door clicking quietly shut behind him.

The king nodded at the two leather chairs beside the window. "Please. Sit."

She obeyed, her weak knees only too happy to find a resting place. The king sat down opposite her. All at once, she was struck by how much they looked alike. The bright blue eyes, high cheekbones, dark ebony hair her brother wore short and cropped.

"You are Melaina's daughter."

"Yes." She cleared her throat as the response came out faint, raspy. "You knew her?"

"I was only eight when she left, but yes, I remember her. My mother and she were very close."

Until my mother had an affair with your father and was thrown out of the palace.

"Aristos has filled me in on your conversation. On your claim that my father is your father."

She lifted her chin. "It isn't a claim. He is."

"Forgive me," he said bluntly, "if I cannot accept that as fact. For over two decades your mother has kept you a secret, but now when my father is nearly in his grave, she's seen fit to speak out. *Why?*"

"She was afraid I would be taken from her. She didn't want my life marked by her mistake. She thought I would be better off with her, rather than carry the stain of my illegitimacy. But your father's heart attack hit her hard. I think she realized she had made a mistake in denying me my birthright."

He raked a hand through his hair. "So you came here tonight to…"

"Know my father. To know you and Stella. I—" Her gaze held his vivid blue one. "I don't have any siblings. I don't want anything else. I have a life in Stygos that I love."

He narrowed his gaze. "You can't be so naive as to think everything will stay the same if it's confirmed you are a Constantinides. You will be of royal blood. Third in line to the throne."

She shook her head. "I don't want any of that. I am not so *naive* as to think I would be welcomed into this family given the nature of my birth."

The king's eyes flickered. "There is a…*complexity* to the situation. But if you are telling the truth, the blood that runs through your veins cannot be denied. It must be dealt with. Acknowledged. But that is dependent upon us having the facts. A DNA test will need to be performed."

She nodded. Had assumed as much would be required. Knew she couldn't have expected more. So why did her insides sting so much?

The king stood up. "I must get back to my guests. You'll understand, given the need for security at the moment, if I have you escorted to a suite where you will remain for the evening. In the morning, we will address this."

"Of course." She got to her feet.

The beautifully appointed suite she was shown to at the back of the palace overlooked the formal gardens. It was done in gold and a soft moss green, the shimmery, wispy fabrics of the sweeping brocade curtains and the romantic overlay of the big canopy bed like something straight out of one of the fairy tales she'd devoured as a child.

When a maid showed up minutes later with a beautiful silk nightgown and inquired if she needed anything else, Alex fought back the hot tears that gathered in her eyes.

She'd accomplished what she'd come here to do. She *would* see her father. But what she wanted in this moment was for her brother to have believed her.

She assured the maid she had everything she needed. Unable to sleep, she wandered out onto the terrace. The band, whose lazy serenade had been drifting through the open windows of the ballroom, stopped playing. Then there was only the buzz of the cicadas as she contemplated row after row of perfectly tended, riotous blooms in the floodlit gardens.

A quiet knock reached her from inside the suite. Frowning, wondering who it could be at this late hour, she padded inside and inched the door open. Standing in the dimly lit corridor stood the princess, still clad in her silver gown.

"I had to come."

Alex stared at her sister. The princess's startling blue eyes were counterbalanced by a wide mouth and the high cheekbones that were a signature of her mother's aristocratic haughtiness. Arresting rather than classically beautiful, Stella stared back at her, all of her earlier poise stripped away, her carefully applied dramatic makeup standing out in stark contrast against the pallor of her skin.

Her quick intake of breath was audible. "*Thee mou*, but you two look alike."

"Who?"

"You and Nik."

Alex swallowed hard, a tightness gripping her chest. Her legs felt unsteady, consumed by the emotion of the day, as if one more blow would fell them. She forced herself to move past it, stepping back to allow her sister in.

Stella slipped inside and shut the door. "The party just finished. I hope I didn't wake you."

"I couldn't sleep."

"I expect not."

They regarded each other in silence, wariness and shock

filling the air between them. She searched her sister's gaze for the mistrust her brother had displayed, finding only bemusement and curiosity in return.

"The king told you I was here?"

"Of course not." The princess's lips curved in a wry smile. "At least not willingly. Nik is too protective for that. I overheard him and Aristos talking."

Her lashes lowered. "He is suspicious of me."

"My brother has to be cautious. He has a million grenades being lobbed at him every day with King Idas's descent into lunacy."

Alex bit her lip, chewing uncertainly on flesh she'd already made raw. "You don't doubt my story?"

"When you look more like Nik's sister than I do?" The princess shook her head. "My father's affair with your mother was common knowledge. I think we've all lived with the possibility that something like this might result from his indiscretions. Although for it to happen now is a bit...*startling*."

"I didn't know. I only found out a few weeks ago."

"Nik told me." The princess regarded her silently. "I hope you are not disappointed. My father is an imperfect man. A great king, but an imperfect man. Manage your expectations. Do not expect him to be warm and fuzzy."

"I thought my father was dead," Alex said quietly. "I'm not sure *what* I'm expecting."

The princess's golden-tipped lashes fanned her cheeks. "I can't imagine how you must feel. To find this out now."

Alex exhaled an unsteady breath. "Confused. Bewildered. I'm angry my mother lied to me. I feel...betrayed. And yet I know she did it for the right reasons. She wanted to protect me. How can I be angry about that?"

"Easily." Stella waved a hand around them. "She denied you this. Your birthright."

"Is it?" A vision of her beautiful, serene village filled her head. "I love my life in Stygos."

"You are a royal," Stella countered. "A Constantinides. You could have had the world at your fingertips. Instead she took that away from you."

Had she? Or had her mother given her the safe, loved existence she'd always known?

"Perhaps it's about destiny," Alex said. "Maybe mine was to live the life I have."

"Perhaps." A glimmer filled the princess's eyes. "The life of a royal has its challenges. I will be the first to admit that."

The reticence in her sister's voice stirred her curiosity. "But the benefits outweigh the challenges?"

"I'm not sure that's an analysis I can make." Stella's lips firmed. "Do I think it's my destiny to be where I am? Yes. Would I have chosen it if given the choice? That is the million-dollar question."

It certainly was. The cicadas buzzed their musical song as a silence stretched between them. Stella set a probing gaze on her. "I saw you dancing with Aristos."

Heat rose to stain her cheeks. She had been hoping *that* part of the evening would go unnoticed. Her inappropriate behavior had been uncharacteristic for her, foolish, particularly damning in light of her mother's scandalous reputation.

"It was a mistake," she said quietly. "I was nervous. I'd had a couple of glasses of champagne…"

"Aristos has that effect on women." The princess's mouth twisted. "A word of warning. He takes what he wants until you are too blind to see the danger. Before you know it, you're hooked. Then he turns you loose."

She was clearly speaking from experience. Alex set her jaw resolutely. "It's never happening again. After I talk to my father, I'm going home."

The princess regarded her silently. "I just met my sister," she said softly. "I find I quite like the idea of having one. It would be a shame to lose her so quickly."

A throb consumed her chest. It grew with every breath, threatening to bubble over into an emotion too big to contain. Stella seemed to sense it, the thread that was close to breaking inside her. She stepped toward the door. "It's late. We can talk in the morning. Better you get some sleep so you have a clear head as all of this unfolds."

And then she was gone, her exotic perfume wafting through the air. Alex's mouth trembled as she shut the door. She stood, leaning against it, every muscle, fiber, of her body shredded, spent.

As all of this unfolds. She was terribly afraid of the chain of events she had set into play tonight. A force she couldn't retrieve. That in needing to know her father, by taking a risk that was so totally outside of her nature, she had not only stepped outside her safe little world in Stygos, but entered one that could consume her. A world her mother had done everything she could to protect her from.

CHAPTER THREE

Two DAYS PASSED, and with them Alex's premonition came true. As the blood test undertaken by the royal physician was rushed through the requisite channels, rumors of her presence spread through the palace in a flurry of gossip only a royal household could induce.

By the time the results of the test were delivered to the palace, confirming that Alex was indeed King Gregorios's daughter, the gossip had spilled to the press, who were demanding confirmation.

Nikandros made it clear they could not wait long in issuing a statement from the press office confirming her as a Constantinides. The longer they waited, the more time the press had to speculate on the story, something the family didn't need as the country fretted about a coming confrontation with its sister island.

It was with this daunting scenario in place that Alex met her father for the first time. Accompanied by Stella to his suite in the west wing of the palace where the king was convalescing, they were told Queen Amara was out for the day. Alex had the distinct impression she was avoiding her as the scandal she was.

Propped up against a pile of pillows, his leathery olive skin lined and craggy from almost four decades of rule, her father was pale beneath his swarthy complexion, his abundant shock of white hair looking out of place on a man who was clearly fighting what might be his last battle.

Stella left. Frozen with indecision, Alex stood in the

center of the room. The king opened his eyes, directing a brilliant beam of Constantinides blue at her. "Come. Sit."

She forced herself to move, perching on the chair drawn up beside the bed. Ruthless, arrogantly sure of his rule, beloved by his people, perhaps one of the last of an impenetrably powerful group of monarchs, her father was vastly intimidating.

He scoured her face. "You look like your mother."

She nodded. Cleared her constricted throat. "We are very much alike. In looks and disposition."

"How is she?"

"She is fine. We run a hotel, my family. It does well."

The king nodded. Contemplated her silently. "You are a Constantinides. As Nikandros will have told you, that gives you royal status. A place in this family."

"Yes." She drew a deep breath. "That's not why I'm here. I came to see you. To know my brother and sister. Not to cause upheaval."

His eyes darkened, a hint of emotion entering his gaze for the first time. "Upheaval there will be. Many mistakes have been made on all sides." He lifted a hand. "I am not long for this world, as you can see, so it will not be up to me to right my wrongs. My wife will come to terms with this. It is *you*, Aleksandra, who must step up and claim your rightful place in this family."

Her hands, clasped together in her lap, tightened their grip, nails digging into her flesh. No outpouring of warmth from this man. No declarations of love for his own flesh and blood. No regret he hadn't been there for her...

Stella had been right. She shouldn't have gotten her hopes up. And yet she had.

Knowing her father was alive had instilled a sense of longing in her. To have that illusion her mother had painted for her, that of a father who'd be excited at the thought of her. Perhaps not the one who would have taken her fishing, who would have taught her about boys, because that was not who this man was to her. Perhaps one with whom she could have forged a more mature bond. One who would have considered her a gift he'd never known he had.

It knocked the wind out of her, the hope. A dull, dead throb pushed its way through her.

"Did you love her?" she rasped, needing to know if her mother's feelings had ever been returned. Needing to salvage *something* from this.

The king fixed her with that steely blue gaze. "I cared about your mother, but no, I did not love her. A king's priority is to the state. There is no room for anything else."

She could have begged to differ, because clearly her brother was very much in love with his wife, but the frozen feeling invading her, siphoning off the emotion that threatened to corrode her insides, made it impossible to speak. Buffered her from more pain.

She had come for answers and she had gotten them. Perhaps not the ones she'd wanted, but answers nonetheless.

Alex spent the rest of the day attempting to wrap her head around the decision she had to make, the media circus going on outside the palace walls making her imminent decision a necessary one.

The decision should have been easy, because she'd never wanted to be a princess. Her visit with her father had been desperately disappointing. Her loyalty lay with the promise she'd made to her mother and the hotel they ran. No one could *force* her to become a royal, but the fact that she was third in line to the throne wasn't a minor detail she could ignore.

What played a larger role in her decision-making were her brother and sister. Now that she'd met her siblings, it was hard to think of walking away from them. But what did she know of being a royal? A princess? It was perhaps the most important question of all, one only Stella could answer.

She pulled her sister aside before dinner and picked her brain. Was life as a princess the endless round of royal engagements and charitable commitments that it looked from the outside, or was there more to it? Would she have any freedom to chart her course, or would it all be decided for her?

Stella answered honestly, which seemed to be her default setting. Yes, it was much as she'd described. But there was an opportunity to own the role, as she herself had proven.

Armed with the full scope of Stella's perspective, not that it cleared her confusion much, she and her sister joined her family for a predinner drink. Nik and Sofía were already enjoying a cocktail, minus two-month-old Theo, their infant son, who was with his nanny. Queen Amara walked into the salon just as the butler handed Alex a glass of wine. All eyes focused on the elder queen as she made her way toward Alex. Breath stalling in her throat, she dropped into a quick curtsy, entirely forgetting Stella's instruction that it wasn't necessary.

The elder queen waved it off with a flick of her hand. "You are a member of this family now."

Am I? I haven't made that decision yet. Her brain rifled through safe things to say. "It's an honor to meet you, Your Majesty."

The queen inclined her head. "Amara will be fine."

The cocktail hour seemed stilted and forced compared with the previous night. When they sat down to dinner, Alex was thrilled to have a knife and fork to devote her attention to.

"When will you be announced as princess?" Queen Amara directed her cool green gaze at Alex. "I would expect soon, given the throngs of media driving us all mad."

"I—" Alex put down her fork and knife. "I haven't actually decided yet what I'm going to do."

Queen Amara lifted a brow. "What do you mean, *decide*? You are third in line to the throne."

"I have a life." Alex lifted her chin. "My mother and I run a hotel together."

"You are a royal. There is no *decision* to be made. Duty says you take your place as an heir to this country."

Her mouth tightened. "My *duty*," she said, "is to my mother and the business we have built together."

Silence fell over the table. "This is all a great deal for Aleksandra to take in," Nik interjected smoothly. "Of course we hope she stays. She is family."

Her stomach tightened at the warmth in her brother's gaze. It was as if he'd been withholding emotion until it was safe to express it. It unraveled something inside her, an almost unbearably bittersweet swell consuming her chest. She picked up her water glass and drank, giving in to the impossibility of eating.

By the time the meal mercifully came to an end, she felt raw in her skin.

Nik headed off to a meeting in his palace office, Sofía upstairs to bathe Theo, Stella out for a drink with a friend. After a call home, an emotional conversation in which her infinitely wise mother told her she needed to do what was right for her, her voice breaking as she did, Alex curled up in the library to think. Process.

But when even that peaceful setting felt too stifling to think, she headed for the magnificent palace gardens instead. If she was going to find a clear head, it would be there.

Aristos emerged from his second visit to the palace in under a week with a strong sense of foreboding that Akathinia had yet to see its most trying times. The king had requested the unusual after-dinner meeting to inform him he'd called all his troops up for active duty after Carnelia had summoned its own reservists, signaling a possible imminent aggression by Akathinia's sister island.

Nikandros had requested he release the rest of the financial commitment he had made to the armed forces to enable the country to protect itself, to which he had agreed.

His head mired in what this would mean for his casino, a potentially devastating delay in breaking ground next month looming, he headed for the front doors of the palace. He was almost there when he saw an undeniably eye-catching female in a white dress headed across the foyer in the opposite direction. *Aleksandra.* He would have recognized that sweet derriere anywhere.

He couldn't deny he'd been wondering how she was. The apprehension in her eyes when he'd walked out of the library the night of the ball had been playing on his mind. Why that was, why he felt in any way protective toward her, was a mystery to him. Out of sight, out of mind wasn't a cliché in his world; it was how he lived his life.

If you didn't invest in people, it was impossible for them to disappoint you. For *you* to disappoint them.

His step faltered on the gleaming marble floor. *Don't do it, Aristos. You already crossed the line with her once. You have far too much on your plate already.* If the $2.5 billion Akathinian hotel and casino didn't get off the ground, his personal investment went down the drain with it, a loss that could threaten his company's existence.

Why he then found himself changing direction and heading toward the back of the palace was anyone's guess. Aleksandra had been headed toward the gardens. He chose the path toward the spectacular fountains and pool at the center of the sprawling botanical extravaganza and found her perched on the wide lip of the fountain, looking like something out of an Impressionist painting.

Wearing a simple white summer dress that left her tanned legs bare, her silky dark hair caught up in a high ponytail, her full mouth pursed as she contemplated what appeared to be a significant issue, she looked good enough to eat. Undeniably edible to his far-too-jaded palate. And yes, this, he decided, had been a big mistake.

Too late, however, as she looked up at him, blue eyes widening. "Aristos."

"Sit," he said as she scrambled to her feet, brushing off the back of her dress. Dumping his jacket on the edge of the fountain, he sat down beside her. Noted the distance she put between them as she returned to her perch with an amused pull of his mouth.

She slid him a wary look from beneath dark lashes. "Overseeing your security again?"

"Meeting with the king. I saw you on the way out. I thought I'd check to see how you're doing."

"You who hunted me down, seduced me to find out what I was up to, then threatened to put me in handcuffs?"

His amusement intensified. She was embarrassed about what had happened between them. About the undeniable chemistry they shared…

"Let's get one thing straight," he drawled. "I *kissed* you because you are one hundred percent my type, angel. Petite brunettes with insane curves do it for me. *Seducing* you would have required more privacy than we had. Although I am not against a bit of voyeurism to add some spice to a sexual encounter, a palace party would *not* have been the occasion I'd have chosen."

Her mouth went slack. "You would not have had the chance, regardless."

He raked his gaze over her pink cheeks, ramrod-straight spine, the faint dip of cleavage the neckline of her dress revealed. The flush staining her chest. The thin material did little to hide the peaks of her breasts thrusting against the material, hard delectable buttons he knew would be a rosy slice of heaven. All signs of a very obvious sexual attraction between them.

"No?" he challenged silkily. "When was the last time you let a man put his hands on you like that?"

She shut her mouth and kept it shut this time. He reached out and ran the pad of his thumb down her cheek, her silky soft skin hot to the touch. "Just for the record, I *am* disappointed, Princess. Your little bombshell that's rocking the country has put you on the endangered species list. Not to be touched under any circumstance. Unfortunate, when that kiss proved just how spectacular we would be together."

Alex hauled in a breath, her insides collapsing into a pool of molten heat. She knew she should be saying something smart back to this unholy man who appeared to say and do anything he deigned, but she was too busy imagining what it would be like to be seduced by him in the true sense of the word. *Hot, forbidden, unbearably exciting.*

He was insufferable, had done a job on her sister, who refused to admit it, and still, she couldn't deny she was disappointed, too.

She pulled her gaze away from the dark vortex it was sinking into. Lifted her chin. "Stella isn't petite and curvy."

His gaze narrowed. "Exchanging notes, you two?"

"She saw us."

"We were like oil and water." He lifted a shoulder. "It was a mutual decision."

She gave him a long look. "Is there a woman on earth you haven't taken to bed?"

"Dozens," he drawled. "Too bad you'll be one of them."

She blinked. "*Wow.* Just wow."

He threw her the most charming of smiles. "I *did* come out here to see how the meeting with your father went."

She considered him. He looked sincere. "It was…fine."

"Fine?"

"I wasn't expecting an outpouring of affection."

"So what did you get?"

She hesitated, unsure if she should be sharing this with him. He spread his hands wide. "The king trusts me with his military secrets…"

"He was aloof," she said. "Abrupt. He said he cared for my mother but never loved her. That there is no room for love when you are married to the state."

"It's a tough job," Aristos offered. "Your life can't be your own."

She was sure that was true. "My mother painted me a rosy picture," she said in response to his continued study. "She led me to believe she and my father were very much in love, to protect me I know, but I think I would have preferred the truth."

"Love is a concept we've all been trained to believe in. It gives us false expectations of our relationships, convinces us monogamy, a lifelong, eternal love, is the norm, when in fact it isn't. Human biology, the study of other animals, tells us that. And yet we continue to aspire to it because we think it's the right thing to do. The golden ideal."

She absorbed the depth of his cynicism. "So you don't believe love exists?"

"No, I don't. I think love is actually sexual attraction disguised as something deeper. When that fades, as it always does as evolutionary history has proven, people drift apart."

She didn't want to believe that was true. Didn't want to let go of her idealism so easily. For if the king of England was willing to abdicate for Wallis Simpson, didn't true love have to exist? If Scarlett and Rhett's passion could survive a civil war and two marriages, wasn't a once-in-a-lifetime bond possible? If it wasn't, if it was only the stuff of fiction, then all her daydreaming during her stolen moments with a book had been an exercise in foolish fantasy.

She wasn't letting *him* burst yet another bubble, she decided. Not at this particular moment when she needed some illusions to hang on to.

"So what happens now?" he prompted.

"I have to decide whether I want to be a princess."

"There's a decision there? I thought every woman wanted to be a princess."

"Not me. I love my life in Stygos."

"So you're going to spend the rest of your life living in a tiny coastal village when you could be exploring the world?"

"Lots of people would give their right hand to live in Stygos." She couldn't help the defensive note in her voice. "What's wrong with a quiet life?"

"Nothing if you're fifty. What do you *do* there?"

"I run my family's hotel with my mother."

"And when you're not working?"

"I see friends or I...read." Her chin rose at his mocking look. "The hotel business is a 24/7 occupation."

"I know that, Alex. I run several of them. I also know what hard work it is if you own a small property and have to do everything yourself. You could leave that behind. Hire someone to work with your mother."

She shook her head. "My mother and I made a pact when my uncle turned the hotel over to her to run. We promised we would always be a team, that we would do this together. To leave her seems like a betrayal."

"But these are extraordinary circumstances. Are there other family members who can help?"

"My cousin, yes. Much of my extended family is involved in the business."

"Then you shouldn't worry about it."

"But I *love* it. I love getting to know people. I love making them happy for a week or two out of their year. I love being busy. If a person has a calling, this is mine."

"Because you don't know any differently." He eyed her. "I think it's wonderful you and your mother are so close. But someday you're going to have to break free of that bond."

She bit her lip. "You think it's a crutch for me?"

"Your words… What I'm saying is that life is about living. Having the freedom to live. When was the last time you went out on a date?"

A long time.

"That long, huh?"

"A year. Since my boyfriend and I broke up."

"And he was?"

"Sebastien Soukis. He's the butcher from the next village."

An amused glint entered his eyes. "Don't tell me… He knows how to *handle* a woman."

Her mouth tightened. "It's a very respectable profession. Whereas yours is questionable."

"Right." He nodded. "I steal unsuspecting people's money."

"I didn't quite put it like that."

"Yes, you did. So what happened between you and Soukis?"

"I—" She waved a hand at him. "We decided to split."

"You were bored."

"He asked me to marry him."

"And you said no because?"

"It didn't seem right. I couldn't…envision it."

"Because it would have been too limited a life for you. You are young, Aleksandra. If you accept this opportunity, you'll have a life, experiences few people will ever have. A life most people would give their right arm for. What's the hesitation?"

"The fear of the unknown." The anxiety that had been

plaguing her all day tipped over into an honesty she couldn't contain. "I'm happy with my life. What if I do this and I'm terrible at it? What if I give up everything and find out it was a big mistake?"

"Then you go home," he said softly. "But don't shy away from this opportunity because you're scared. It's harder to run from your fears than face them. Trust me."

She took in his ultra-confident, ever-so-self-assured persona. "That's easy for you to say."

"Why? Because I'm a powerful man? It wasn't always that way. I've had my own conflicts. Two different roads I could have taken. It would have been easy for me to take the simpler one, the one I was drifting toward at the time, but it wouldn't have been the right one. Taking yourself out of your comfort zone is the most powerful thing you can do."

That intrigued her. "What were they? The two roads?"

"Ancient history." He tucked a wayward curl behind her ear. "My point is you should take the jump, Princess. Privilege is a powerful thing. Use it wisely and it'll be worth the reward."

His touch sent an electric impulse firing through her. She sank her teeth into her bottom lip as a shiver of reaction chased up her spine. If she'd been hoping her visceral response to him was a product of the champagne that night, she'd been sadly mistaken. She hadn't touched but two sips of her wine before dinner, and still she was so aware of him she wanted to jump out of her skin.

His dark, sinful gaze commanded hers. Dragging his thumb along her lower lip, he nudged the tender flesh free of the bruising grip her teeth had taken of it. "Stop fretting," he murmured, "and make the decision."

She got all tangled up in him. In the intimate claim he was staking on her mouth, the pad of his thumb stroking the vulnerable curve of her lower lip. Her stomach went into free fall as heat built between them, wrapped itself around her like an invisible force she was helpless to resist.

Her mouth went dry, anticipating, *willing* the kiss she knew would be worth the insanity of allowing it.

He brought his lips to her ear, his warm breath playing across her skin like an intimate caress. "That would be breaking the rules. I have a great deal of incentive not to do that, angel."

Rolling to his feet, he picked up his jacket. She hauled in a breath, attempting to corral her racing pulse.

He tossed his jacket over his shoulder, his gaze on her. "The woman who sashayed her way into the royal ball insisting on speaking to the king would see this for the opportunity it is. Guess you have to decide which one you are."

Turning on his heel, he sauntered off into the night. She watched him go, head spinning. Inhaling a long, steadying breath, she digested the encounter. Attempted to determine the veracity of what he'd said.

Had she been missing out on the world in Stygos? Would she regret it if she stayed there? It had been easy to work most of her waking hours, to devote herself to the family business in the pursuit of a better life for her and her mother. To satisfy her need to know the world by burying her nose in a book, lost to the adventures she'd found there. *Safe.*

She thought about everything that had happened since her mother revealed her shocking news. How it had seemed as if the world had shifted beneath her feet. How everything she'd thought she'd known seemed like an illusion, and everything she hadn't, her earth-shattering new reality.

She had a choice. To take back control of her life or have it control her. Because one thing was for sure; Nik had been right. Her life would never be the same no matter what she decided. She was a royal. A princess.

Perhaps it was not duty that would inform her decision, but a desire to truly know herself. To expose herself to the world and see what it reflected back at her. To stop living her life on the pages of a book and instead experience it for real.

Did she have the courage to take another huge leap? To leave everything she knew behind? If she did, what would she find when she got there?

CHAPTER FOUR

"How does it feel to be a princess, Aleksandra?"

Terrifying. Bewildering. Like I have no idea what I am doing.

Alex swallowed hard, her knees knocking together as she looked out at the sea of reporters crowding the palace gardens for the official announcement of her appointment as Her Royal Highness, Aleksandra, Princess of Akathinia. Packed into the center of the labyrinth of neatly trimmed hedges in the Versailles-style gardens, there were hundreds of them toting cameras of all varieties, the buzz in the air palpable as they waited to grill the new royal.

It was the largest showing of a press contingent since the king and queen's wedding the year before, a showing Alex had been well prepped for since making her decision to take her place as a Constantinides. And still her tongue was cleaved to the roof of her mouth, a rivulet of perspiration running down her back under the handpicked designer dress she wore.

Stella gave her an encouraging look from her position beside her, Nikandros flanking her other side. Taking a deep breath, Alex addressed the reporter in the front row.

"I'm still getting my feet wet. Perhaps you can ask me that again in a few months and I'll have a better idea."

"What is your role going to be?" the reporter followed up. "Do you have any causes you currently support?"

She was still trying to figure that out. It was her number

one point of anxiety, in fact, since getting the hotel in the black had been her "cause" to date.

"I'm working through that," she said. "More to come."

"Why hasn't the world known about you before now, Aleksandra?" another reporter called out. "Is it true your mother kept your birthright a secret?"

"That's a personal matter I won't comment on."

"What about your father's affairs? Is it possible there are more of you out there?"

"Again," she said, "I won't comment on my family's personal affairs."

"How do you anticipate handling the glare of the spotlight?"

"Day by day. Like any new job, I will have to learn my role. Luckily," she added, nodding at her siblings, "I have my brother and sister by my side."

A reporter directed a question at Stella about her new sister. Alex took the opportunity to breathe. A tall figure leaning against a tree behind the reporter claimed her attention. *Aristos.*

Clad in another of his bespoke suits, he sent her pulse scattering. *What was he doing here?*

"Aleksandra." The reporter turned her attention back to her. "Overnight you have become one of the country's most eligible women. Are you single or in a relationship?"

"I'm single."

"What are you looking for in a potential husband?"

"I'm not looking," she countered. "I have enough on my plate at the moment. But if I were, integrity, intelligence and kindness would be high on the list."

Aristos's mouth kicked up at the corners. Heat flamed her chest, rising to her face. *Diavole*, but why was he here?

"It's rumored the duke of Catharia is quite taken with you. Perhaps there's potential for a romance there?"

Her eyes widened. The duke had been seated beside

her at an official dinner two nights ago. He was charming and attentive, and she'd enjoyed his company, but since she'd been told to keep a low profile considering today's announcement, she hadn't given him any encouragement. Perhaps also because her head had kept going back to her encounter with Aristos in the gardens. Charming as he might be, proper like the duke, he was not.

"The duke is lovely," she said, lifting her chin. "But nothing to report there."

The press flung a dozen more questions at her, covering everything from her life in Stygos to her favorite color. When they had exhausted anything that could be considered remotely interesting, a reporter in the middle of the pack directed a question at Nikandros.

"What do you make of the fact that Carnelia has called its reservists up to active duty?"

Her heart jumped. *It had?* Nikandros moved to the mike. "I think we're doing everything we need to be doing to ensure Akathinia's safety, now and in the future.

"Are you anticipating an invasion by Carnelia?"

"We hope it won't come to that."

The media peppered the king with a series of questions on the Carnelian situation. Alex kept her gaze on the press corps rather than on the man making her feel utterly conspicuous. *Naive* and conspicuous.

The press conference thankfully came to an end. The PR liaison appeared to usher them back into the palace. Stella stopped to talk to a reporter she knew, while Alex continued on with her minder, anxious to get away from the frenzy.

Aristos appeared at her side, his long strides easily gaining him even with her as she walked toward the palace. "Well done," he murmured. "You took the leap."

His designer stubble was thicker than usual, giving him a wicked, pirate-like appearance. It kicked her insides into high gear despite her better sense. She gave him her best haughty princess look. "Surely you didn't come just to laugh at me?"

"You've been busy," he noted. "Taking my advice. A duke already... And no, angel, I didn't come to see your performance. I have a meeting with the king."

Oh. Her stomach dropped. And why was that? She needed to be staying away from him, not courting his attention.

"There is no duke. He was seated beside me at dinner. That's all."

"And you flashed those baby blues at him and he didn't stand a chance."

She turned to face him. "I was *not* flirting."

"You don't have to. You're a natural." He gave her a pained look. "But kindness, integrity and intelligence? Really, Alex? You might as well have posted a neon sign inviting all the Sebastiens of the world to come running. That was *not* what I meant when I said expand your horizons."

She narrowed her gaze. "That is just...*rude*. Any woman would be lucky to have Sebastien."

"Except you," he pointed out. "You're far too hot-blooded for that, Princess."

"Oof." She stuck her hands on her hips. "I tell you what. The next time I need dating advice I *won't* come to you and your heartless reputation. I'll figure it out myself."

"Ouch." He pressed a hand to his chest. "Heartless. That hurts."

"I'm sure you are withering away inside." Noting that Stella was directly behind them, she pressed her lips together and flung him a cool look. "Enjoy your meeting, Mr. Nicolades. Good afternoon."

She turned on her heel and swished her way through the palace doors. Stella caught up with her in the hall. "What was *that*?"

"Nothing." Absolutely *nothing*.

Alex headed to her meeting with her cultural adviser. A familiar anxiety worked its way through her as she sat through two hours of princess training. How was she ever going to get this all right? It all seemed unnecessarily complex and…*antiquated*.

She reminded herself why she was doing this. Stella and Nik were amazing. She hadn't been able to resist the chance to get to know them better. And perhaps because Aristos had been right. She had been playing her life safe with a whole world out there to explore.

Which didn't mean she had to pay attention to *him* and his condescending, provocative comments. If she was going to master this princess thing, she couldn't allow Aristos Nicolades to distract her at every turn.

Firming her mouth, she gave her adviser her undivided attention.

Aristos was still smiling over his confrontation with the feisty Aleksandra when he walked into the king's office. Nikandros's personal aide ushered him into the inner sanctum without delay.

"Thank you for coming," the king said, gesturing for him to take a seat in the sitting area by the windows. "I need a favor."

Aristos's always-opportunistic side perked up. The more goodwill he could bank with the king, the better. Construction on the casino on the shores of the Akathinian harbor would mean surprises—rude, *expensive* surprises a royal influence could help smooth out. Accelerate solutions for.

"Always," he said, crossing one long leg over the other and sitting back in the chair. "What can I do?"

Nik sat down opposite him. "My sources say Idas may make a move on this country as soon as his armed forces are at full strength. As such, we need to shift to a high alert."

His stomach plummeted. It was the worst-case scenario he'd hoped would not come to pass. What would his investors think of such an uncertain environment? A war that could destabilize the region? Would they jump ship? Let their nerves get the better of them?

A knot formed in his gut. He had doubled down on this one. Put the better part of his personal fortune up to back this casino. If it failed, *he* failed.

Your ambition will be the thing that fells you, Aristos, unless you learn to control it.

"Aristos?" Nik was frowning at him.

He shook his mentor's words out of his head. "Sorry, yes?"

"I want both princesses off the island. Stella has a good friend she can stay with in Athens. I need you to take Aleksandra to Larikos."

He blinked. The king wanted him to take his stunningly beautiful, unwittingly sexy, *very* innocent half sister to his private island in the Aegean Sea for safekeeping?

"Of course I'm happy to do whatever you require," he said carefully, "but of all people, Nik, you must know *I* am not a babysitter."

The king fixed his laser-sharp blue gaze on him. "I'm not asking you to babysit Aleksandra. I'm asking you to provide a safe place for an heir to the throne until this is settled. The security on Larikos is impenetrable."

Because he had a casino there where some of the richest men in the world came to play…in a few weeks, actually. "She would be better off with Stella," he suggested. "Wouldn't that be more reassuring for her?"

"Akathinian law says I can't have two heirs to the throne, however distant, together in a situation like this."

He firmed his mouth. "I'm not the man for the job, Nik.

I am scheduled to be all over the globe the next few weeks. I'll ask friends to host her."

Nik pinned his gaze on him. "That you are precisely *not* the man for the job is exactly why I want her with you. It's the last place anyone would think to look for her."

It was not a request. It was a command if he valued the casino license he'd spent the past five years chasing.

"All right. When?"

"Friday."

"Friday?"

"Friday," the king said firmly. "And, Aristos?" Nikandros shot him a deadly look. "I don't think I have to say that Aleksandra is off-limits."

Aristos absorbed the underlying message. The insinuation he wasn't good enough to fraternize with a royal. It had been this way, too, when rumors of his and Stella's brief liaison were circulating. He would have hoped with all the respect he and Nik had gained for each other over the past year working together, the king's opinion of him might have changed. Yet clearly, Nikandros still considered him beneath his family's blue blood.

His jaw hardened, his fingers tightening around the arms of the chair. He'd made an art of not caring what anyone thought of him. It had been a necessity in the life he'd led, in the business he operated in, with the checkered past he carried with him that was always in danger of resurfacing. The tightness in his chest suggested he hadn't quite perfected it.

"Consider it done," he said curtly, rolling to his feet. He had bigger fish to fry than a princess, including a flock of investors whose hands needed holding. A plan B to execute he'd hoped he'd never have to use.

His ambition wasn't the problem. It was the universe and how it was unfolding that was messing him up. Fortunately, he'd never met a calamity he couldn't conquer.

This casino *would* happen. His business would not fail. He was never going back to where he'd come from. *Ever.*

Alex and Stella were summoned to Nik's office after dinner, an unusual request given that the king had been burying himself there of late, forbidding interruptions. Alex rose from her chair, darting a look at Stella. "Do you know what this is about?"

Stella shook her head. "No idea. Could be Carnelia."

The worried look in her sister's eyes had *her* worrying. She followed Stella down the hall to Nik's office, where her brother waved them into chairs.

"You heard the speculation today about Carnelia calling up its reservists," he began, without preamble. "We have confirmed this is true. We have no idea whether Idas is bluffing or planning to make a move on Akathinia."

Her heart dropped.

"He wouldn't dare," Stella exclaimed. "He knows the world is against him."

"I'm not sure he is in his right mind. Regardless, I think it's prudent to remove both of you from the island for the next little while until we can determine the situation."

"And Sofía and Theo?" Stella asked.

"They stay. Sofía refuses to leave."

"Then I'm staying, too," Stella said. "I'm not leaving you."

Nik's gaze softened. "I appreciate the show of solidarity, but I can't have the three heirs to the throne here. Nor do I have the energy to fight with you. My wife is making it hard enough."

"He won't do it," Stella said. "He's bluffing. Why doesn't Kostas talk some sense into his father? What is *wrong* with him?"

"The crown prince remains noticeably absent. Do what

I ask. *Please.* We are well defended, Stella. It's just a precaution."

Stella clamped her jaw shut. Nodded. "We can stay with Cynthia, then."

"You can. Aleksandra will stay on Larikos with Aristos. It is written in our laws the heirs must be separated in a time of war."

"Aristos?" The sisters said the word in unison. Stella's jaw dropped. "Why?"

"Because his casino is impenetrable. She'll be better protected there than anywhere else."

"I'll go home," Alex interjected.

"I'm afraid that's impossible. You would be too vulnerable there."

She bit her lip. "What about my family? I can't leave them unprotected."

"I will make sure they are looked after."

Her head spun. This was *madness.* "I really don't think this is a good idea."

"Why?" Nik threw the question at her with the look of a man who'd just about reached his limit.

She exchanged a meaningful look with Stella. "I just… don't."

Nik's gaze moved between the two of them. "If you have something to say, spit it out."

I can't be marooned with Aristos on his private island for Lord knows how long when I am clearly, inadvisably attracted to him.

Unfortunately, the next day, she was packing to do exactly that.

CHAPTER FIVE

LARIKOS, ARISTOS NICOLADES's private island in the heart of the Aegean Sea, sat to the east of Greece. Surrounded by sparkling cerulean-blue water, it comprised seventy acres of priceless real estate upon which Aristos's much-buzzed-about, invitation-only high-roller casino was situated, as well as his private estate and guest residences.

"The famous Great House." Aristos's pilot pointed at a massive, sprawling thatch-roofed structure that sat perched on a hill overlooking the sea. He listed off names of celebrities, politicians and royals who'd stayed in the €10,000-a-night suites. "The villas," the pilot said, "for those who wish for more privacy, are the structures scattered down the hill."

Alex absorbed the spectacular aerial view, then sat back in her seat, fingers clutching the armrests. Having never been on a plane before in her life, let alone a helicopter, she had been torn between terror and exhilaration as they'd made the trip from Akathinia to the place she would call her home for the foreseeable future.

She had, of course, not been about to tell Nik about her disreputable behavior with Aristos the night of Stella's party, thus the inevitable conclusion of her conversation with the king. There had been time only to call her mother to assure her she would be taken care of before she and Stella were whisked away from the palace for safekeeping.

Safekeeping. Her stomach dropped as the helicopter dipped and made its way toward the landing pad near the

Great House. She was worried about her family. Worried about what Idas would do. Sure she should be there by their sides and not *here* hidden away with the man she'd practically thrown herself at the other night.

Being uprooted again, separated from everything she knew under the most worrying of circumstances when she'd only just begun to settle into her new life, had been disconcerting. Unnerving. As if she were frozen midjump.

She wanted to know she'd done the right thing in abandoning the life she'd loved, to know everything would fall into place. Instead she'd been handed complete uncertainty.

Her fingernails sank deeper into the leather as the pilot set the helicopter down on the landing pad. A tall, dark male stood waiting, his shorts and T-shirt whipping in the wind. *Aristos.* Her stomach did a flip-flop of a whole other kind. She'd thought maybe he'd send one of his staff to greet her, hadn't even known if he would be here. Just because he was hiding her away didn't mean he had to play host.

Aristos pulled the door of the helicopter open and greeted the pilot. It gave her an opportunity to inspect him in casual clothes during the short exchange that followed.

The show began with the close-fitting T-shirt that stretched taut over his broad shoulders and cut abs, not an excess centimeter of flesh in sight, and ended with the most impressive set of powerfully built thighs and calves she'd ever seen. Pure masculine perfection that hinted at the fact that the rest of him she *couldn't* see was just as mouthwatering as what was on display.

He eyed her as he lifted her down to the ground. "You okay? You look a bit green."

"Fine," she managed past a churning stomach. "I've never flown before. It was an adventure."

He kept his hands on her waist. He smelled like earthy sexy male today, with a hint of sandalwood as opposed to his usual spicy urbane sophistication. Little pinpricks of heat flared beneath her skin as he studied her face, multiplying with unnerving speed until she was drowning in her awareness of him.

"You mean you haven't flown in a *helicopter* before," he corrected.

"No. I haven't flown, period."

His eyes widened. "Surely you've been outside of Akathinia?"

"Only to the Greek islands. Perfectly accessible by boat and automobile."

He looked at her as if she were a creature from Mars. She stepped back, pressing her palms to her flaming cheeks. "There's been no opportunity. You said it yourself. Running a small business means you have no personal time. Every time we hired someone we thought was reliable enough to take part of the workload on, we found we couldn't trust them."

"Staff will always be your biggest headache and asset. Has your cousin stepped in to help your mother?"

She nodded, a throb filling her chest. *Taken her place* was how she saw it.

"How did your mother take the news?"

"Not well." Her mother had been trying to mask her feelings, but she knew she was devastated by her decision, feeling the loss of their bond as much as Alex was.

His gaze softened. "No one said taking the untraveled road was easy."

Brutally hard was more like it. She was getting the sense this new life of hers was going to be a one-challenge-a-day kind of affair.

Aristos picked up her suitcase and headed toward the Great House. She trotted along behind him, half running to keep up.

"I'll show you to your room. Get you settled. Yolande,

my manager, is going to give you a tour of the island this afternoon. She'll be your point person for anything you need while you're here."

Because she was a pain in the neck to him. Because having her here was a huge inconvenience, likely the last thing he needed with a potential war delaying his casino.

"Thank you for opening your home to me," she said, drawing alongside him. "But please, don't feel like you have to play host. I'm sure you have a million things to do."

His dark gaze glittered in the sun. "Unfortunately, you and I are stuck together, angel. I am your official babysitter for however long it takes Carnelia to realize Akathinia can't be taken."

She blinked. *That could be weeks. Months.* "Surely you have to travel… You can't stop doing business because of me."

"I'm going to do it from here. I'll do day trips if I need to."

"That's ridiculous. Your business is all over the world. I don't need a babysitter. I can take care of myself."

He stopped and looked down at her. The warmth in his gaze had vanished, replaced by a cold black stare. "The king has entrusted you to my care. You are a potential target in these games Carnelia is playing should they elect to make a point out of you. You are therefore my responsibility and will do what I say while you are on this island. Understood?"

An icy feeling invaded her. She wasn't sure if it was this vastly intimidating version of Aristos that did it, or the fact that he'd just marked her a kidnapping target.

She swallowed past the lump in her throat. "You don't really think Idas would come after me or Stella, do you?"

"No. I think it would be highly unwise of him. But taking chances would be equally foolhardy."

Right. She shut her brain down before her imagination

ran wild and considered, instead, Aristos's distinctly cool demeanor as she followed him up the steps of the sprawling, airy structure with its incomparable views of the sea. Gone was the incorrigible, devilish version of him she'd come to expect, replaced by the Aristos she'd met the night of the ball.

Apparently Aristos ran hot and cold. Too bad the last time he'd run hot she'd practically begged him to kiss her.

"You can pretend I'm not even here," she suggested. "Better yet, put me to work. I've managed a hotel. I'm sure there are things I can do."

"There are no guests here right now. And what," he tossed over his shoulder, "would the king think of me putting you to work?"

"He'd be happy that you've kept me occupied?"

"I don't think so, Princess. Not going to happen."

She and Aristos were alone on this island. Well, them and a few dozen staff, likely. She digested that fact as she followed him up to the third level.

"When do the next guests come?"

"I'm not hosting any groups while you're here for security reasons. With the exception of an invitation-only poker game in three weeks. Everyone attending is a personal acquaintance of mine, each one thoroughly screened with background checks."

Oh. Her heart plummeted as she stepped onto the third-floor landing. His gaze speared hers. "What's the matter, Princess? Afraid to be alone with me?"

Not in your current chilly state, no. She lifted her chin. "Why would I be?"

Their gazes clashed, black battling with blue. "Oh, that's right," he said silkily. "You're looking for 'integrity, intelligence and kindness.' You'd best go find your duke."

She pressed her lips together. "I already told you, there is no duke."

He turned and strode down the hall. She followed, staring at his broad back. What had she done to annoy him? Or maybe he was simply irritated with the situation?

Her confusion fell to the wayside as she stepped into the ridiculously large, high-ceilinged bedroom Aristos had entered at the end of the hall. Her suite at the palace had been straight out of a fairy tale, but *this*, this was something else. Paradise, perhaps.

The three walls that enclosed the room were a cream-colored canvas for the bright, beautiful island art that covered it. The final wall that faced the sea comprised floor-to-ceiling glass with sliding doors that opened onto a terrace, offering a spectacular view of the endless blue horizon.

With that jaw-dropping perspective as a backdrop, the suite descended into sumptuous, hedonistic heaven. Gauzy cream-colored curtains were drawn to either side of the dark wood canopy bed. A decadent-looking daybed enjoyed a perfect view of the sea, promising hours of reading pleasure.

"Aristos," she breathed. "This is incredible."

"Nothing too good for the princess in residence."

She ignored the gibe, too caught up in the magic of the ethereal room. "I love it. It's perfect."

"Good. My bedroom is there," he said, pointing to the terrace beside hers. "So I can keep an eye on you. My office is in the casino. Yolande will show it to you this afternoon so you know where to find me." He turned and gestured toward the writing desk tucked away in the corner of the room. "There's a secure phone and internet line. You're not to use your usual devices. Turn them off and keep them off."

She bit her lip. "Okay."

"As for meals," he continued, "the chef on the main level is at your disposal. As are any of the water sports and activities. The staff are available to accompany you. The only thing you will *not* do is swim unaccompanied. The undertow can be strong with the *meltemia*."

"I'm Akathinian, Aristos. I was born on the water."

"The rule still applies." He leaned against the wall. "A few things. You will notice armed guards posted on the island. They carry *big* guns. There's no reason to be alarmed—they're for the protection of the guests we host, many of whom are VIPs whose safety is a top priority. To that end, there is no way on or off this island without my personal knowledge and approval. There's a three-mile blackout around us, meaning no aircraft or boat crosses it without my team's knowledge."

Armed guards with big guns and a no-fly zone? What had she walked into?

"Is that really necessary?"

"Yes. More than one of my guests have been kidnapped and held for ransom. It won't happen here."

That word again. *Kidnapped.* She wiped a palm over her brow.

"I thought we could have dinner. Sometime around eight?"

She met his cool gaze with one of her own. "I meant what I said. You don't need to babysit me or keep me company. I'll be fine."

"I have time tonight." He headed toward the door. "Enjoy your tour."

She tried to. Yolande was lovely, and Larikos *was* paradise. Whereas Stygos relied on its wild, natural beauty to attract visitors, its way of life virtually unchanged from a hundred years ago except for the most necessary of modernizations, Larikos was sleek and sophisticated.

From its sensational tropical gardens to the world-class clay tennis courts to the Romanesque-inspired casino, the island sparkled with an opulence that was reflected in every detail. But all that sophistication only made her pine for home. For beaches that were just as beautiful, views just as spellbinding. Her mother, who must be terrified as to what was to come…

She would have given anything in that moment for everything to be back to normal, where life had made sense. But nothing was normal anymore—perhaps never would be again. Her world as she knew it had vaporized, and she felt completely, utterly adrift.

Aristos spent the afternoon in his office, immersed in conference calls to make up for where he was supposed to be had he not been babysitting a princess. Almost all of them were to pacify nervous investors about the Akathinian situation, including one of his biggest, Russian oligarch Dimitri Smirnov, who had seemed even more wily and elusive than ever, marking the Akathinian political situation as "worrying" and refusing to give him a firm commitment that he would stick with him.

He'd therefore put plan B into motion: using his shrouded-in-secrecy, much-anticipated, invitation-only annual poker game on Larikos to keep everyone happy.

He never messed with the sanctity of the game. Any of the business contacts he mixed with the pros were players who could hold their own, but this year, he had invited all his key financial backers, including a wild card in Dimitri, so he could keep a finger on the pulse of them all. He only hoped it wouldn't destroy the game.

Frustration swirled through him, singeing his skin. *Too many calls. Too many uncertainties.*

He slammed a fist on his desk. If he'd been in Moscow as he was *supposed* to be, he could have talked Dimitri into a commitment. Instead he was here, protecting a princess he was supposed to have dinner with in a few minutes. Entertain. He could only hope the Russian would take the bait and attend the game he'd long coveted a place in. It wasn't looking promising.

Noting the espresso he'd spilled in his tirade, now eating up the pages of a report on his desk, he uttered another choice word, grabbed some napkins from his drawer and started mopping it up. He refused to consider the graveyard of men who'd conquered Vegas and Atlantic City, only to end up destitute, consumed by their own greed.

That would never be *him*. He wadded up the napkins and threw them in the trash. His risk had been big but calculated. Bold but not foolhardy. He couldn't imagine a day when he forgot what it was like to wonder where his next meal was coming from, where he was going to sleep that night. It was the kind of desperate clawing existence that was burned into your brain forever, no matter how far your star shot up in the sky—no matter how distant a memory it became.

It was something every human being knew if they were reasonably self-aware. Everything you had could and would go away in the flash of a neon Sin City sign if you didn't keep your eye on the prize.

Just as his own life had once vaporized in the space of a head-poundingly hot Athens night in which heated accusations had been delivered, ultimatums issued and decisions made that could never be taken back.

He pulled himself out of his ruminations with a scowl. It was the thinking of a man who hadn't slept enough, who had subsisted on a diet of far too much coffee and too little food today, his hesitation in heading toward sustenance with only one name: Alex.

She'd had another of those lost, disoriented, utterly out-of-her-element looks on her face when she'd arrived. And why wouldn't she? She'd been ripped away from her family once again with a war looming in Akathinia, clearly no happier to be here with him than he was to be stuck with her.

He had been cold with her, yes, stifling what seemed to be his natural desire to comfort her, because it was the only way to manage the attraction between them.

The women he dated were sophisticated creatures with the benefit of a world of experience. Who knew the score with him. Who didn't complain about his lack of commitment because they'd known from the start it was never coming, and for the time they were together, he provided them with everything money could offer.

It had been that way since his early days in Vegas. Since he'd discovered that having money meant an endless supply of women who cared more about his wealth than the man behind it. Which had suited him just fine. After his parents' disastrous marriage that had seen his mother kick his father out after years of vicious fighting and his infidelity, he had no desire to ever enter into the illusionary institution of marriage.

Carin, his PA, stuck her head in his office and prompted him about dinner. He rolled to his feet, threw his laptop into his briefcase and headed toward trouble. Trouble he was going to neutralize. If Aleksandra's innocence wasn't enough of a deterrent for him to keep his hands off her—which quite honestly, he suspected it might not have been under different circumstances—the fact that the king had warned him off her was.

Which meant keeping Alex at a distance by whatever means necessary.

Showered, changed, dressed in jeans and a T-shirt, and still not entirely free of his filthy mood, Aristos found the princess waiting for him on the terrace of the Great House. The fragile image she cut against the dusky pink-and-red sky, a tiny figure versus the big, scary universe she'd been thrown into, tugged at his heart. He was, after all, partially responsible for encouraging her to embrace this brave new world.

"I should have told you the dress is casual here unless we're having a formal night."

She turned around, a wry smile curving her mouth. "And here I was just getting used to the training that's been drilled into my head. *"Refined dress on all occasions, Aleksandra. Classy yet understated."*

He could have told her that on her, with her perfect curves, anything looked sexy. That the very proper turquoise wrap dress she had on only made a man want to unwrap her as a most fortunate present. That her hair, plaited down her back, elicited the same urge. But since his mind was supposed to be out of the gutter when it came to Alex, he declined to go there.

He crossed to the wine bucket sitting on a table and began uncorking the bottle of sparkling white. "You aren't supposed to let them turn you into a robot."

"I'm not." She frowned. "It's just…there are rules. So many rules. Standards to uphold. It's all a bit much."

"Stella knows her own mind." He filled two glasses, waiting for the fizz to die down to top them up. "Use her as an example."

She took the glass he handed her, a contemplative look on her face. She was curious, he knew, about his relationship with Stella, but there was nothing to tell. They had been two consenting adults scratching an itch, whereas Alex was vulnerable, *emotional*.

He surveyed the dark circles that lined her eyes, their red-rimmed appearance. Her emotions were not his concern; her safety was. But the tug on his heart at her obvious misery was too strong.

"So," he drawled, "what's eating you? You've been off since you arrived."

Her eyes widened. She opened her mouth to say something, then clamped it shut. "I'm worried about my mother," she said quietly. "I feel like I should be there by her side, not here, as lovely as it is."

A twinge of guilt assailed him. He should have been more reassuring earlier rather than scaring the hell out of her. "There's no need to be concerned about the political situation in Akathinia. The minute Idas makes a move, which I still have doubts will ever happen, the world will respond. Akathinia is too important a symbol for its former colonial interests to watch its democracy be compromised."

She gave a doubtful nod. "I suppose you're right."

"I am," he said firmly. He lifted his glass. "To your leap. May it lead you to many fantastic adventures."

She lifted her glass to his. Remained pensive as she drank.

He cocked a brow. "What?"

"I feel like I've been ripped away midjump. I was just getting settled, trying to figure out what I'm going to do, and then all *this* happened." She pursed her lips. "I need to find my 'thing.' My cause to support. All I've learned so far is how to smash a bottle of champagne against a ship without maiming myself and how to cut a ribbon without making it fray. It's making me crazy."

He leaned against the railing, balancing his glass on the top. "Rome wasn't built in a day. Have you been given any direction? Perhaps Stella has some ideas."

"She took me on a tour of the new youth center the charity she represents is building. It's very impressive."

"Youth Compass?"

She nodded.

"I'm on the board of directors. It's a good organization."

She crossed her arms over her chest and tucked her glass beneath her chin. "What got you involved with them?"

"A percentage of the profits from each of my casinos is diverted to the homeless and youth organizations in the cities we operate in."

Her blue gaze turned assessing. "So the big bad casino mogul has a heart."

"Oh, I wouldn't go that far, Princess. Corporate social responsibility is smart business."

"And that explains the staff you've hired to work on Larikos who were living on the streets? Who had no particular skill when you hired them and now they're the head groundskeeper and the engineer who maintains your solar project?"

He must remember to tell Yolande to cut down on the personal anecdotes. "It's an issue society has to tackle."

She pointed her glass at him. "I need something like that."

"You need to be personally invested in it. What turns you on, Princess? Gets those creative juices of yours flowing?"

Her face went a rosy pink. He knew exactly where her head was, because it was where his was. Where it was every time they were within five feet of each other. *In bed, satisfying their intense sexual curiosity about each other...*

"Other than me, angel," he drawled. "We've already established that as a nonstarter."

Her eyes widened, a deep flush staining her chest to match the one in her cheeks. "You are insufferable sometimes, you know that? And just...*deluded*."

His mouth curved. That was better. Feisty he could handle. The sad puppy-dog look, not so much.

"Insufferable, yes," he agreed. "Deluded, I'd argue. You were craving a follow-up to that kiss that night in the gardens as much as I was." He moved his gaze over her soft, pink, very consumable mouth. "You aren't exactly subtle with your signals."

Her mouth thinned. "Wanting something and acting on it are two different things. In actuality," she said, pinning her gaze on his, "the duke *is* much more my type than you. There is a civility about him I enjoy."

"Really?" The blatant lie, yet another slight from a Constantinides insinuating he was beneath their blue blood, evaporated his good humor. *His rules.*

"If I took that glass out of your hand right now," he said, holding her gaze, "picked you up and carried you upstairs to my bedroom to do exactly what we both want to do, you would *not* be complaining, Princess. You would be *begging* for me to finish it. And *that* is the truth."

She blinked. "That would never happen."

"You want to *try me*, angel?"

Color leached from her cheeks, leaving behind a pallor that told him he'd gone too far. And still the nerve she'd hit pulsed in his jaw, making it difficult to summon the self-control he knew he needed.

"Perhaps you're right," she acknowledged quietly. "But hormones don't have a lot to do with common sense, do they?"

She slayed him with that one simple line.

Alex almost turned on her heel and skipped dinner with Mr. Hot-and-Cold after that display. Her deeply ingrained good manners, however, wouldn't allow her to do it. Mr. Hot might be back, but she could manage him. Manage *this*. At least she thought she could.

What plagued her as Aristos seated her at the candlelit table for two on the edge of the large formal dining room, in the cooling breeze of the sea, was that she was afraid he was right. That if he'd done what he'd said, she might not have protested, might have been unbearably excited instead. And that was a head-scratcher, given what she knew of Aristos's reputation. Given the fact that Sebastien hadn't been able to persuade her into bed with him during their yearlong relationship, her boyfriend resorting to asking her to marry him in an attempt to get her there.

She wasn't sure what she'd been waiting for. Lizzie and Darcy's spark-strewn courtship? Gatsby's grand obsession with Daisy? Or perhaps the inescapable attraction she felt toward Aristos—as if a magnet kept pulling her toward him no matter how hard she tried to escape. Made worse by the fact that now she knew he had a heart. That the man behind the stunning good looks was one who cared enough to pluck two strangers off the street, one in Rio and one in Las Vegas, pay for their education and give them a job on Larikos, his most exclusive property. A second lease on life...

He liked to paint himself as the devil beyond redemption, but he was far more than that. It was dangerous to even let herself go there; she knew it as she lifted the glass Aristos had refilled and sipped her wine. But she couldn't seem to help herself.

"What about your reading?" he said, breaking the silence that had fallen between them with a return to their earlier discussion. "You said you love to read. Why not literacy as a cause? Youth illiteracy is a major issue. You could team up with Stella on activities..."

She thought about it. She had never thought of her reading that way, as a privilege, when in fact, it was. For her, a story that transported her to another world had always been a part of her life. Her mother had taught her English as a little girl, considering it an invaluable skill. The nook in her family's hotel where guests left their discarded books had become her gold mine. And yet not everyone had been granted that privilege, even for critical, life-sustaining purposes.

"I love that idea," she said quietly, recognizing it as the peace offering it was.

"Then use the time here to pick a short list of organizations you might like to work with."

She would. She attempted to focus on her salad as a

silence fell between them again. More peaceful this time. But she found her appetite had waned. Or was it just difficult to concentrate on anything with Aristos sitting across a candlelit table from her? When it looked as if he had been poured into the white T-shirt and dark blue jeans he had on, his current level of intensity only making him that much hotter.

"Enough about me," she said, offering a peace branch of her own. "What's been keeping *you* up at night?"

An amused expression crossed his face. He sat back in his chair, his wineglass cradled in his palm. "The list is too numerous to bore you with."

"You have to be worried about the casino."

"Yes, but much of that is out of my control. All I can do is try to convince my investors there is no need to worry."

"And is that working?"

"Most seem fine. One in particular, Dimitri Smirnov, a Russian oligarch, seems shaky. I've invited him to come to Larikos for the poker game, so I can firm him up."

Her stomach sank. "Which you could be doing now if you weren't babysitting me."

He shot her a reproving look. "We've had this conversation."

Yes, but she hated that she was standing in the way of something so important. "How does the game work?" she asked. "Who gets to come?"

"I thought you found my profession distasteful, Princess."

She sighed. "Hector Rigatos, my best friend's father, lost all his family's money gambling in Las Vegas. I know it's an extreme case, but that's why I have a problem with gambling. And could you *please* stop calling me Princess? You know very well I dislike it."

"There are some unfortunate cases like that," he acknowledged. "Most people, however, learn to enjoy responsibly.

As for calling you Princess," he drawled, "I like it. I find it reminds me *who* you are."

As if he'd forgotten for one second. She shook her head. "How long has the game been going on?"

"Five years. The players like it because it's private. They can let their hair down. What happens on Larikos stays on Larikos, so the saying goes. Social media, any type of reporting, is banned."

She could only imagine what happened when men, money, power and competition got together. "Do they get up to very naughty things?"

"Sometimes. Nothing that's fit for your ears."

"Please. How much is the opening ante?"

"One hundred thousand US dollars."

Thee mou. "And by the end of the game?"

"Last year it went as high as one point three million. We ended with twenty million worth of chips on the table. Which," he advised, "is not a public figure."

Her head spun. This was *beyond* fascinating. Unlike poor Hector Rigatos, these men knew what they were doing.

"You give a percentage to charity," she guessed.

"Yes."

"Do you play?"

"Sometimes."

She'd bet he'd be the most formidable of players...bet he looked smoking hot doing it.

She pursed her lips, regarding him thoughtfully. "So how do we get Dimitri Smirnov here?"

"You mean how do *I* get Dimitri here?"

"I can help. I can do some research... We've done some really great events at the hotel to draw in high-profile guests."

"I run a poker game, Princess, that's all. Dimitri's always wanted to play. We'll see if he bites."

She chewed on her lip. "Why the hesitation, then?"

"It's his wife's birthday that weekend. I already offered them an extended stay on Larikos to celebrate. If that doesn't do it, I'm not sure what will."

She couldn't imagine what woman in her right mind would turn down a week on Larikos. When they weren't in captivity, of course... But maybe, she thought, her brain percolating, there was more, something personal they could offer Dimitri Smirnov's wife as a birthday present. An experience she couldn't find anywhere else.

Her lips curved. Research was what was needed. Good thing Aristos had given her a laptop. If she just so happened to surf up some information on Mrs. Smirnov that might help, was that a crime?

Aristos eyed her. "No, Alex."

"No, what?" she countered innocently, spearing a tomato with her fork.

The conversation remained on neutral, innocuous topics after that, topics Aristos seemed to handpick to keep their interaction in a safe zone. She played along with it because she knew it was the smart thing to do.

After dinner, he walked her upstairs, likely to ensure she was ensconced in his heavily guarded fortress for the night. Each step along the long hallway, toward a bedroom, *another* foreign existence that was now hers for weeks, perhaps months, brought with it a low-grade anxiety. She didn't want to be alone. She didn't want to be *here*. She wanted her life back. Which one she wasn't sure.

"Can I get you anything?" Aristos asked as they reached her bedroom door.

It was the wrong question to ask. She bit her lip, hot tears burning the backs of her eyes. "No," she said huskily, blinking them back. "I'm fine."

He reached out and traced her cheek with the tip of his finger. "Alex—"

She flinched. Shut herself into her room with a murmured thanks and told herself to stay there before she did something really, really stupid.

Aristos stood outside Alex's room for a good minute, torn between the desire to go after her and comfort her and knowing exactly where it would be headed if he did. In the end, he turned and went to his own room, where he answered a few last emails from his overseas teams.

The storm rolled in about an hour later. One of those vicious assaults that came out of nowhere and packed the wrath of God. It brought with it a stunning display of thunder and lightning that seemed to shake the walls of the Great House, although in reality it was far too well-built for that.

He got up from his chair on the terrace, went inside and checked that the lightning strike detection system was activated. When he saw that it was, he poured himself a drink and went back outside to watch the show.

White and gold streaks of lightning arced across the inky black tropical sky, jagged, intricate fingers of pulsing light that dazzled the eye with their spectacular patterns. The thunder grew louder with every pass, its powerful roar shaking the floorboards beneath his feet. Faster and more frequent it came until there was virtually no pause between the cracks of thunder. It must be close. Almost directly overhead.

He wasn't sure what alerted him to Alex's presence on the terrace adjacent to his. The storm was too loud for him to have heard her. She stood, wrapped in the white silk robe the resort provided its guests, her arms wrapped around her. A bolt of lightning zigzagged through the sky, hitting the water not a hundred feet from them. It illuminated Alex's pinched white face. *She was terrified.*

Turning on her heel, she ran inside. He headed toward

her room, expecting the door to be locked. She must have forgotten to do it, because the handle turned and he walked into the room, colliding with a wall of frightened female.

"Whoa." He gathered her into his arms. "What's going on?"

"Th-that strike," she stuttered. "It was too close. It was—"

"We're fine." He ran a soothing hand down her back. "We get these storms all the time."

"So do we. I *h-hate* them."

"They sound worse than they are."

"What if it hits us?"

"We have sophisticated detection systems. We'd be on it in a minute."

A crack of thunder made her jump. She was shaking so hard her teeth were chattering. Uttering a curse, he set her away from him, walked to the bar and poured her a finger of cognac. Drawing her down on the sofa, he pulled her into his arms, her back nestled into his warmth.

"Drink," he said, pushing the tumbler into her hands.

He was staying for a few minutes until she calmed down. That was it.

She curled her fingers around the glass. Took a sip. "That's really strong."

"It'll calm your nerves."

She took another sip. He smoothed his palm over her hair, still bound in the tight plait. It made him hurt to look at it. "This *has* to be giving you a headache."

"My hair was a little wild. I'll take it out before I sleep."

He undid it for her, sliding the elastic from the bottom of the plait and methodically working the braid free with his fingers as the storm continued to roll over them. "Why are you so frightened? A bad experience with a storm?"

"My uncle Rasmus was hit by lightning when I was a little girl. He was a fisherman. He went out on his boat one morning, early, very early, when a storm like this rolled in. Luckily, one of his fellow fishermen saw it happen. They took him to the hospital, but his left side was paralyzed. He could never man a boat after that."

"That must have been frightening for a little girl."

She nodded. "I know the chances of it happening are one in a million, that it's an irrational fear, but you think if it can happen once, it can happen again."

He worked the last section of the braid free. Her hair fell around her shoulders, like warm silk under his hands. It was beautiful. She should never wear it up. If she were his, she never would.

The bizarre train of thought made him scowl. He never kept women around long enough for them to be "his." Where was *that* coming from?

The beats between thunderclaps lengthened, the bright bursts of lightning lessening in their intensity, becoming fewer and further in between. He moved his fingers to her scalp, his slow, easy massage meant to distract.

"Aristos…"

"Mmm?"

"Your two roads. What were they?"

His fingers paused in her hair. "Ancient history. Like I said."

She twisted around to look at him. "If it's ancient history, why won't you tell me?"

"Because it doesn't matter anymore."

"If it doesn't matter, why can't you tell me?"

Because it involved intimate details of his personal history. Because barely anyone knew the story. Because she would know him if he did.

And yet she'd had the courage to tell him her deepest fears. Had taken a massive leap few would ever have had the courage to take in leaving her life to become a princess.

Surely he could tell her a story that didn't matter anymore? That had nothing to do with the man he was now?

Or perhaps had everything to do with the man he was now…

He pulled her back against his chest, his hand returning to the satiny fall of her hair. "When I was sixteen, I was living on the streets in Athens. Running with a gang. I was distanced from my family for various reasons, bitter about the lot the world had handed me and headed down a very dark road. My mentor, David Tennyson, one of the men who revitalized Las Vegas, was visiting Athens. He was in front of a restaurant one night, smoking, when I attempted to relieve him of his wallet.

"He was too street savvy to let that happen. But instead of turning me in to the police, he wanted to know why I was on the street. I told him my story. He saw something in me, saw past the anger and the bitterness. He wanted to help me, he said, but only if I gave up my lawless ways. He handed me twenty one-hundred-dollar bills and a business card that night and told me if I wanted to learn the casino business to come to Las Vegas."

She twisted around to face him. "You went."

He nodded. "You only get a chance like that once in your life."

"Or never." She sank her teeth into her bottom lip, a habit he found himself once again wanting to correct. Only, he knew how he'd do it, and there wasn't anything innocent about the vision that filled his head. "That's quite a story."

"It wasn't a match made in heaven. Not in the beginning. I had a lot of baggage I had to work through…anger issues. David has a tough background himself. He wasn't about to put up with me breaking the rules. There were no easy shortcuts, I would come to realize. The path to success was a great deal of hard work."

"What's your relationship like with David now?"

He thought about it. "Like father and son, really."

"And your own family? Did you reconcile?"

"No."

"Why not?"

"Some paths you can never reconcile."

His tone was hard. Final. She opened her mouth, then closed it. "Does David come to your poker game?"

"Yes." He held her gaze. "That story is not for public consumption, Alex. David and I are the only ones who know the history, the only ones who ever will."

"I won't tell a soul," she said. "Thank you for telling me. I understand now about the choices you were speaking of. How difficult it must have been for you to choose. How we all have a choice."

He tucked a chunk of her hair behind her ear. "What were you upset about earlier?"

"I was homesick." She waved a hand at the sea. "It's so beautiful here. Your island is incredible. But it makes me think of Stygos. How much I miss it…"

"Did you call home?"

"Yes. It's just…I feel lost. I want to know I've made the right decision giving up my life. I *think* I have, then the doubts creep in."

"That's when you have to stay the course," he said firmly. "It gets harder before it gets easier, just as I said about my early days in Vegas. Once you've passed the point of no return, doubt is normal. It's what you do with that doubt, the strength of spirit you put behind it, that makes the difference."

Her lips curved in a heartbreakingly vulnerable smile. "You are wise, Aristos Nicolades."

"Along with being insufferable and rude?"

"Yes." Her smile grew. "Perhaps you are my David. Pushing me on the right course…"

He shook his head. "I identify with your struggle, that's

all. I know how hard it is to walk away from everything you know. To tell yourself you're doing the right thing even when it's terrifying. Even when you *know* it's right."

Her gaze darkened. Stayed on his. The moment hung, suspended between them. She was soft and warm against him, still within the circle of his arms, that brilliant blue gaze of hers eating him up.

"Alex," he growled, blood drumming in his ears. "We have rules."

"I know." She whispered the words even as she drifted closer. Her scent, a mix of jasmine and something he couldn't put a finger on, wound its way around him. To have all those curves within touching distance, that amazing mouth close enough to touch, *taste*, was playing havoc with his common sense. His rules.

She had drifted so close now, her lips were mere centimeters from his. He could have stopped the madness; he was still in possession of all his faculties, whereas Aleksandra was on the far side of vulnerable and clearly not. Perhaps because of that and not in spite of it, he didn't push her away. Didn't listen to the voice in his head asking him if he had a death wish.

She was seeking comfort. Surely he could keep it to a kiss? One kiss. Then he'd put her to bed, *alone*, and be on his way.

He could do that.

He let his breath mingle with hers. "What's the matter, angel? Don't have the guts to take it all the way?"

She brushed her mouth against his. He almost groaned out loud at the pillowy softness of it…how good she tasted.

The alpha in him couldn't leave it like that. Capturing her jaw in his fingers, he took control. Firmer, lusher, the kisses went until they had fully explored the texture and shape of each other. Then he slid his tongue into her mouth and rediscovered the intoxicating flavor of her. She tasted like peaches and pears from the wine she'd consumed, as heady as he remembered.

His blood heated, his body responding to the perfection of their connection. He should stop it now. Do what he'd said he'd do. But when he moved to disentangle them from each other, Alex protested and moved closer. "Soon," she murmured against his lips.

Soon? She was too tempting beneath his hands not to touch. Too tempting *to* touch. *A couple more minutes*, he told himself. Max.

Sinking his hands into her waist, he lifted her up so her knees came down on either side of his thighs. It gave him access to all of her. Perhaps not so smart.

Moving his lips to the smooth column of her throat, he satisfied a burning need to taste more of that silky smooth skin with lazy openmouthed kisses that revealed she tasted that good all over. *Christe mou.* Lust coiled low in his gut at the sweet, honeyed flavor of her. It made him wonder if she'd taste like that between her thighs…like some kind of forbidden ambrosia he'd never get to sample…but desperately wanted to.

He traced the pulse that raced at the base of her throat with his tongue, absorbing her indrawn breath.

"Aristos." His name on her lips sounded so sexy with the perfect roll of the *r*, all the blood in his body fled south.

"You are so perfect," he murmured, dipping lower to the hollow between her breasts. The plunging neckline of the robe gave him easy access to the beginning of those beautiful round curves. Succumbing to temptation, he slid his fingers beneath the silk, rasping his thumbs across the twin hard peaks. Alex gasped and arched into his touch, her breathy moan kicking him low in the gut.

He wanted to look at her, to wrap his mouth around her, to lavish his attention on her naked flesh. Instead he brought his lips back to hers in a kiss that flouted sanity, searched for it even as Alex buried her fingers in his hair, urging him on. Unable to resist those sexy moans, he rolled her nipples between his fingers, teased the aroused peaks even tauter, her answering groan heating his blood.

This is madness. Somewhere deep inside his brain the thought registered, finally clicked with unerring precision. Lifting his mouth from hers, he pulled the silk lapels of her robe together and set her away from him on the sofa. Alex stared at him, a stricken look on her face.

"*Soon* is over," he bit out. "*Soon* was a bad idea."

"Aristos—"

He got to his feet. Hardened his heart against the vulnerability that cloaked her like a second skin. "The storm has passed. Get some sleep."

Turning on his heel, he left before his common sense deserted him completely, his rules in tatters.

CHAPTER SIX

IT WAS NO USE.

Alex set her laptop on the table, swiped up her espresso and sat back in the plush lounge chair, drinking in the idyllic view of an endless blue horizon from her private terrace. Perhaps more caffeine might kick-start her brain into working order, because all it could focus on right now was *the kiss*. Well, not just the kiss. The way Aristos had taken intimate possession of her body *after* the kiss.

She closed her eyes as the memory singed her skin. How utterly and completely lost she'd been…how it had felt as if she were playing with fire but she hadn't cared… the knowledgeable rasp of his thumbs across the peaks of her breasts igniting a need she hadn't known existed…

Her blood pumped through her veins at the memory, warming her cheeks. In the cold light of day she recognized her actions as foolish, inspired by the loneliness enveloping her the night before, by the need to know if that kiss the night of the ball had really been *that* good, that that kind of passion existed off the pages of a book. And perhaps, most of all, because uncovering the Aristos who was so much more than the ruthless casino scion he was made out to be had proved undeniably fascinating. Lethally compelling.

She wondered at the strength of character he must have displayed to get where he was today. Wondered what could have happened in his family to drive him onto the streets. She wanted to feel special because he'd confided something to her he'd never confided to anyone else, but she knew that would be taking her foolishness to a whole other level.

She was sure the Aegean Sea was littered with the emotional corpses of countless women who had crashed and burned in their attempts to get to the bottom of Aristos. Who'd thought *they* would be the one. She would not be one of them. Not when he was the same kind of philanderer as the one who had broken her mother's heart. Stolen her dreams. Left her pining for a love that would never be hers.

That he was fast becoming an anchor for her, that Aristos Nicolades, notorious playboy and ruthless take-no-prisoners force of the business world, was serving as a fountain of wisdom on this new road she was traveling, seemed a rather bizarre development. But last night she'd seen he was far more than the image he presented to the world. She had a feeling it had been only the tip of the iceberg. So perhaps not so crazy after all…

Still, even if all that were true, even if she wanted to know that kind of passion for real in this new, more-daring version of herself, Aristos was the last man she should do it with. The way he'd dumped her on the sofa and left last night should be more than enough incentive to convince her of that. It had been vastly…*humiliating*.

She took another long draw on the espresso, attempting to drown her mortification in the dark eye-opening brew. She would be far better off doing what Aristos had suggested, working on her future, taking back control of her life in constructive ways, than fixating on a kiss.

She spent a couple of hours doing just that, looking at literacy organizations that not only appeared as if they were doing good work but also might benefit from her support as a spokeswoman. She jotted down the names of a couple of charities that looked interesting, then put her research aside for her more pressing task.

Typing in *Dimitri Smirnov* and *wife*, she searched

everything she could find on the oligarch's significant other, Galina Smirnov, a glamorous London-based socialite. The oligarch himself seemed to be of questionable reputation, some of his interests on the shadier side, it seemed. It made her wonder why Aristos did business with him, but that wasn't her mission here.

Working her way through the articles, she unearthed a profile from a glossy magazine. It was rife with information. Skimming her way through the stories of the Smirnovs' legendary soirees, weekend residences and politically notable connections, she found a paragraph about the hostess's not-to-be-missed London dinner parties.

Galina Smirnov entertains with a glamour that harkens back to a golden age, when the jazz greats dominated and the making of a superior cocktail was an art. Cocktail hour at the Smirnovs' is sacrosanct, vodka-based, of course, Galina's collection of the jazz masters incomparable, enjoyed by the guests on an antique gramophone.

Jazz music. Her lips curved. This she could work with. Her mother just so happened to be old friends with the retired jazz legend Nina Karvelas, who had once come to Stygos to sing for their guests at the hotel's grand reopening.

Could she convince Nina to come out of retirement to sing on Larikos as a birthday present for Galina Smirnov? Perhaps the singer would do it if a donation were made to one of the charities she'd spent her retirement working with.

Exhilaration flooding through her, Alex threw on shorts and a T-shirt and went in search of Aristos at his office. His PA, Carin, told her he was booked solid until nine that evening with conference calls. Cooling her heels with difficulty, she headed to the beach, read a classic, took a surfing lesson from the water sports instructor, Diego, then ate dinner by herself. Still no Aristos.

She rose the next day only to be told by Carin that Aristos was in Athens for meetings. *Diavole*. Was he avoiding her because of that kiss? Was he going to avoid her forever?

Humiliation dogging her footsteps, she buried her head in another book to fill the day. By the time dinner rolled around, the thought of consuming another meal by herself didn't appeal. She wasn't even hungry. It felt as though all she'd done was sit around and eat.

She went for a hike up into the cliffs instead, the early-evening air still hot and humid. Sitting on a rock at the top, she took her time enjoying the view, then walked back along the beach toward the Great House.

Passing the tiny little cove off the main resort, a slice of heaven with its pristine white sand crescent bounded by the walls of the cliffs, she was irresistibly tempted. What she wouldn't do for a swim right now, her body grimy and sweaty from the hike. But Diego was off for the evening, Aristos nowhere in sight, the helicopter pad empty. She couldn't even *swim* by herself.

Frustration coursed through her, tightening her fists by her sides. She was a prisoner…a damn prisoner on this island. In this fortress Aristos called paradise. She was an excellent swimmer, there was no risk.

Heat pushed through her, egging her on. She glanced around the deserted little cove. There was no one to see her…

Mouth set, she stripped off her T-shirt and shorts to the bathing suit she had underneath, waded into the heavenly water and sighed. It was perfect.

Aristos landed on Larikos just before nine, the resort sparkling with light against a sky full of stars. Retrieving his briefcase, he thanked the pilot, jumped to the ground and propelled his weary body toward the Great House.

It had been quite the day. Still no word from Dimitri, and a score of meetings with suppliers in Athens persuading them to hang tight, that the ground-breaking for the casino would not be delayed long.

His thoughts turned to Alex as he climbed the stairs toward his suite. He had been ignoring her ever since that kiss, hoping the cloud of vulnerability that surrounded her would fade along with his instinct to comfort her and spill pieces of his past while he was at it.

Kissing her was one thing, a mistake he never should have made, but revealing so much of himself had been worse. If he pretended his past had never happened, refused to acknowledge it, it held no power over him; others couldn't use it as a weapon against his undeniable success. Telling the story to Alex, however, had established it as fact. Brought it into his present. And even though he trusted her and knew it would go no further, it still felt like a chink in his armor.

He climbed the final set of stairs, mouth flattening. The problem was, now he felt guilty. Alex must be lonely. Perhaps she hadn't eaten? Perhaps they could have dinner together? Dinner was safe.

He dropped his things off in his room and knocked on her door. When there was no response, he knocked again. No answer. Turning the knob, he pushed the door open and called her name. Nothing. *Strange.* The dining room had looked empty on his way up.

He went downstairs and found Yolande. "Do you know where Alex is?"

"I haven't seen her since this morning. I thought she might be having a rest."

"She's not in her room. Could she be using the spa?"

His manager made a call. Frowned as she hung up. "She's not there."

Then where the hell is she? An uneasy feeling slid across his skin. Alex had mentioned the cliffs the other night, how she'd thought the view would be amazing. He'd told her the rocks could be treacherous, unstable; it was a hundred-foot drop to the water below; better to do it together sometime.

His unease intensified. Had she gone and done it anyway? Even if she had, it was a short hike; it wouldn't take hours.

"Go ask the staff," he told his manager curtly. "Find out who saw her last."

When Yolande reported back to say no one had seen Alex in hours, a web of apprehension snaked its way around him. His brain flipped to the Carnelians, a thought he immediately dismissed. The island's perimeter was unbreachable. But it remained in the back of his mind, eating away at him, as he called his head of security and ordered a search of the island.

The cliffs worrying him the most, he jumped into a Jeep and headed toward them, his progress hampered by the darkness and the rutted track. Had she fallen? Hurt herself? There were venomous snakes up there…scorpions that could incapacitate a person in seconds.

His brain spun in a million directions. If anything had happened to her…she was his responsibility…under his care.

He hit the gas and the Jeep jumped ahead. This was why he hadn't wanted her here. Why he never wanted to be responsible for anyone. Because every time he had been he'd failed, too caught up in himself to be there when the ⸻on he was responsible for needed him.

⸻ had exhausted every possible scenario in his head, ⸻les in knots as he neared the cliffs, when his pilot called him. He had located Alex. Swimming. In the cove below the cliffs.

What he had strictly forbidden her to do.

He slammed on the brakes, a red mist descending over his vision. She would not have done that. She would *not*.

He sent his pilot home, pulled his security team in, turned the Jeep around and headed back along the track. By the time he reached the path to the cove he was beyond furious; he was apoplectic.

Pulling the vehicle to a screeching halt, he jumped out and headed down the path toward the beach. There, lying on her back, floating in the water, was Alex, illuminated by the light of the moon.

A choked sound alerted Alex to the fact that she was not alone. Flipping onto her front, she trod water, eyes widening when she saw Aristos in a designer suit standing on the shore. Her heart hammered in her chest as he headed toward the water. Surely he wasn't going to… *Thee mou.* Her hand flew to her mouth as he stalked into the sea, a lethally dangerous expression on his face.

She was in so much trouble.

Her tongue, cleaved to the roof of her mouth, could manage only a helpless "Aristos—"

He pushed through the water, sank his fingers into her waist, picked her up, slung her over his shoulder and headed for shore. She gasped, fingers grasping his jacket. "What are you *doing*? Put me down… You're ruining your suit."

He stalked up onto the shore and set her on her feet.

"While you were enjoying your swim, which I expressly forbade you to do, my search team, the entire island, has been looking for you."

"The entire island? Why?"

"You didn't show up for dinner. No one's seen you in

hours. You didn't deign to tell anyone where you were going."

Her heart sank. "I was on my way back. I was just going to be a few minutes more. It's—" she waved her arm around them "—it's so nice here. I told you I'm an excellent swimmer. Isn't this a bit of an overreaction?"

He stepped closer, his powerful body a wall of heat that bled into her skin, sending her heart racing in her chest. "You forget, you are a target, Princess. You are under *my* care. How do you think I'm going to react when you disappear? Do a whistling little stroll around the island calling your name like my dog's gone missing?" He raked his gaze over her face. "There are poisonous creatures on this island. A hundred-foot drop from that cliff. I was worried you'd fallen, were lying somewhere in need of help."

A tight band wrapped itself around her chest. She pressed her palms to her cheeks. "*Lypamai.* I'm sorry... I wasn't thinking right. I was so bored, I didn't—I didn't think to tell anyone."

"Bored?" His breath rasped across her cheek, the intimidating bulk of him pushing her heart rate from fast to furious. "I'll tell you who isn't bored. My pilot, who was finally settling down to dinner... My security team, who've already had a full day's work... Yolande, who is frantic about you."

Tears burned the backs of her eyes. "I said I was sorry. I'm just trying to explain."

"Why?" he demanded. "Why would you disobey my direct request not to swim?"

"I was...frustrated."

"About what?"

"About being here. I have nothing to do. You won't let ⌐lp."

⌐lip curled, wisps of pure fury coiling in his gaze. ⌐w what you need to do, Princess? *Grow up.* Stop whining about being here and thank your lucky stars people care enough about you to want you safe. Some don't have that luxury."

She flinched. Knew he was right, but the humiliation blanketing her lifted her chin. "What about you, Aristos? How grown-up are you being? We share one kiss and you go running for the hills."

"I was *working*, not running for the hills."

"And you couldn't spare five minutes to say hello?" She shook her head. "What are you afraid of? That I won't be able to keep my hands off you? That in my naive, vulnerable state of being, I can't resist you? Because I promise you, I know that kiss was a bad idea."

A smoky, sultry edge laced his furious expression. "Quite the opposite, Princess. I am afraid *I* won't have the discipline to walk away the next time you throw yourself at me. My next move after that kiss would have been to carry you to my bed, remove your clothes and explore every inch of your beautiful body with my hands and mouth to see if you tasted as sweet in all the places I'd fantasized about. And then where would we be?"

Thee mou. Heat uncoiled under her skin, a soft, sinuous unfurling of something molten that scalded her insides. Swallowing hard, she lifted her chin. Halted the insanity. "I know the kiss can't happen again. I would have told you that if you hadn't been avoiding me. As for tonight, I am truly, *truly* sorry for the mess I've caused. It was thoughtless of me."

"Hurricane Aleksandra," he murmured silkily, watching her with a hooded look. "Blows in and sweeps everything up with it."

Her lashes lowered. A shiver moved through her as the breeze swept over her wet skin. Aristos stripped off his jacket and draped it around her shoulders, the brush of his fingertips against her collarbones sending electric shocks of awareness through her. She clasped the lapels together, refusing to show how much he affected her.

"I did," she ventured carefully, "have something I wanted to discuss with you."

He lifted a brow.

"I did some research on Galina Smirnov."

The dark look reappeared on his face. "*No*, Alex."

"Hear me out. I read a profile piece on her. She's a big fan of jazz music."

"And this is relevant why?"

"My mother is old friends with Nina Karvelas."

"*The* Nina Karvelas?"

"Yes. She did a concert once for us at the hotel. She's retired now, but I was thinking she's heavily into her charitable causes. What if you threw a birthday bash for Galina? Nina sings, you donate a sum of money to her charity, everyone wins. It's an experience money can't buy. Exactly what might entice Galina to Larikos..."

His brows came together. "How do we even know Galina is that much of a fan of jazz? People say all sorts of things in profiles to look interesting."

"She has one of the most complete collections in the world. The interviewer was wowed by it."

He rubbed a palm against the stubble on his cheek. "We don't have parties, Alex. It's a poker game."

"So you have an opening night reception before you start playing. This is *Nina Karvelas*. If we could get her to say yes, it would be the coup to end all coups. How could Galina not come?"

"If her existing birthday plans can't be changed."

"So you find out. I could ask my mother to ask Nina in the meantime."

He pursed his lips. Stuck his hands into his pockets.

"Have you heard from Dimitri?"

"No." He gave her a long look. "I need to think about it. And you need to get some clothes on."

They walked back to the Jeep and drove back to the Great House. She changed when they got there, had dinner with Aristos, throughout which she kept her mouth shut, a low profile...until he walked her to her bedroom door that was, when she couldn't resist speaking up.

"What you told me the night before last," she said, looking up at him as he rested a palm against the frame of the door, "about your past...about that strength of character you needed to survive, *that's* what I took away from our conversation. Not the mistakes, not the dark parts, but the courage, the strength you must have had inside you to not only walk away from a life you knew was wrong, but to cross an ocean, to leave everything you knew behind to be something different." She shook her head. "*That* I think is amazing."

His gaze darkened. "So good at building fairy tales, Princess. You're a natural."

There he went again, deflecting praise, admiration. Anything that might be construed as good about him. Refusing to acknowledge who he was beneath the layers, because heaven forbid, someone might get close to him.

She was getting the impression Aristos didn't know how to be intimate in anything but the physical sense. He didn't believe in love, treated his relationships like transactions and preserved that protective shell around himself at all costs because he had been built that way, because whatever had happened in his early years to drive him onto the streets had scarred him badly. Impaired his emotional IQ.

"All right," he said, still striking that same indolent pose, palm against the door. "You win, because frankly, I need the carrot to dangle in front of Dimitri. Call your mother and see if Nina could make an appearance here. But don't make any promises."

A surge of satisfaction flooded through her. *Finally something to sink her teeth into.* Now she only hoped Nina would say yes.

Aristos's gaze narrowed. "This game is a well-oiled machine, Alex. It runs itself. You're making one phone call, that's all."

"Yes." She nodded her head vigorously.

"As for tonight," he said softly, straightening away from the door, "you've signed your warrant. You have now earned yourself a babysitter in the truest sense of the word."

A wary skitter went up her spine. "What does that mean?"

"It means you and I are going to be joined at the hip, angel. I intend on returning you to Nik in one piece."

She pressed her lips together. "That isn't necessary. I've learned my lesson. I won't take a step out of line."

"No, you won't, because I will be there to make sure you don't."

"Aristos…"

He sauntered off down the hall toward his room. "Start thinking of creative strategies to keep ourselves in line, Princess. I'm already off and running."

CHAPTER SEVEN

ALEX MADE THE call to her mother the following morning on a still, quiet Akathinian day in which the Carnelian military exercises continued on the waters bounding the two nations, the only sign anything was amiss. Having assured herself her mother was okay, she explained the situation Aristos faced and how Nina could help.

I owe Nina a call, her mother had said. *I'll see what I can do.*

Setting down the phone, Alex crossed everything. Her impulsive and admittedly recalcitrant behavior last night had had far-reaching consequences. If she could pull this off and Nina said yes, if the Smirnovs took the bait and came to Larikos, she could make amends for her thoughtlessness by planning this party for Aristos. Channel her frustration into something constructive.

True to his word, Aristos was on her like glue. He had lunch with her, dropped by her surfing lesson in the afternoon and joined her for dinner that evening. When he didn't have an eye on her, he had one of his dangerous-looking guards keep vigil. It was all getting a bit old by the next morning when her mother called to tell her Nina had said yes—the singer would consider doing the appearance on Larikos in exchange for the proposed donation to the charity of her choice.

She almost jumped out of her chair with glee, particularly when Nina's charity turned out to be a program that encouraged kids to learn to read through the power of song.

As the singer talked her through it in their follow-up call, Alex's excitement grew. It was exactly the type of work she wanted to get involved in with her love of reading, she'd told Nina. Something she could really make a difference with.

She practically flew over the beach to Aristos's office, one of his professional shadows hot on her heel.

"You've made your point," she said, stopping in front of his desk. "You can call the dogs off now."

"I don't think so," he drawled, sitting back in his chair, gaze lingering on the sweep of her legs in the shorts she wore. "I like having you on a leash, Princess. It gives me great peace of mind."

"Call them off," she said firmly, "or I will phone my mother back and tell her Nina's services aren't required. She said yes, by the way."

A slow smile curved his mouth. "Nicely done."

"I have been negotiating contracts for the hotel for years," she said crisply. "Do we have a deal?"

"Yes. But if you ever wander off like that again, there will be consequences, angel." He crossed his arms over his chest, that lethal gaze resting on her. "Don't let my imagination run wild."

Her lashes lowered, heat shimmering through her. She couldn't help but imagine what those consequences would be. She *should* be ignoring him. Instead she couldn't stop thinking about that fantasy he'd painted of her in his bed, kissing, *tasting* her all over...

"Still working on those creative strategies?" Aristos's taunting gibe brought her gaze up to his. "Looks like it's still a work in progress."

Diavole. She folded her arms. "How are yours coming? You seemed quite interested in my legs when I walked in."

He lifted a shoulder. "I'm a leg man, Alex. I'd have to be dead not to look at yours. Besides, I have strategies."

"Like what?"

"I drew up a list of dinner topics. Wait until you sit down—you won't believe how dry it's going to be. The weather, the spectacular meteor shower that's coming and the fascinating scientific phenomena behind it, what a charitable board member does in all its intricate, excruciating detail so you have your expectations set..." He waved a hand at her. "All guaranteed to have us dying for a good book."

All guaranteed to ensure they didn't have to engage in the intimate type of conversation he clearly preferred to avoid.

"How studious of you," she said. "*My* strategy is to get Galina to bite so I can plan this event and have something to do."

"*If* I let you plan the event."

"Oh, didn't I mention that?" She put her fingers to her mouth. "That's part of the deal."

He gave her a long look. Summoned her into a chair to go through the details. She sat, crossing her legs to give him maximum view, enjoying the power that surged through her when he took advantage of the opportunity to study the scenery with unabashed fascination.

"The exciting thing," she said, "is that Nina's new charity is about engaging youth in education through the power of song. She said we can talk when she comes, and if it seems like a good fit, we could work together."

He tore his gaze away from her legs. "A match made in heaven. That's good news. A happy princess might actually allow things to return to normal around here."

She made a face at him. "Do you want to hear the details? Nina has some requests."

"Go ahead." She went through the list of conditions the jazz singer had detailed. When Aristos approved them all, she left him to call Dimitri.

It was midafternoon, her surfing lesson about to begin, when he found her on the beach, a triumphant glitter in his eyes. "He said yes."

Her heart swelled, a buzz of excitement zigzagging through her. "Will you let me plan the party?"

"Yes." His gaze narrowed. "You own those two hours before the game. Work with Carin on the logistics. She'll have my security team do background checks on Galina's guests. But not another foot out of the box, Princess. You and this game are not mixing."

She gave him a salute. "Aye, aye, captain."

"Also, you are not supposed to be here. You will simply be Alex that weekend. Understood?"

She nodded.

He waved her off to join Diego. She turned and headed toward her instructor, a huge smile on her face.

"Alex?"

She swung around.

"Thank you."

A warm feeling spread through her. "Don't thank me yet. I still have a party to throw."

Alex took her mandate and ran with it. With the party only two and a half weeks away, there was a great deal to do in a short period of time. She created a menu for the party, a special bohemian decor for the bonfire setting and liaised with Nina on her requirements for the performance and her travel and with Galina on her guests and special requests for the evening.

Luckily, event planning was a skill she'd mastered at the hotel. She created a critical path of things to do and checked them off as the days slid by, working furiously to ensure that every detail of Nina's performance would be perfect, because impressing the Smirnovs was so critically important to Aristos.

Aristos continued to work day and night between his spot checks on her, his tension palpable as the poker game approached. He rose with the sun and worked late into the night, more driven than any human being she'd ever encountered.

Now she knew where that drive came from. He had known what it was like to have nothing, had built his business from the ground up, and that business was being threatened.

If the questions in her head grew ever more persistent—about the early experiences that had caused him to cut himself off emotionally from the world, what had happened to send him out onto the streets—she kept them to herself as they tiptoed around their perpetual awareness of each other.

She was finding her feet. It felt good to be contributing. Her mantra was to stay out of trouble, pull off a great party. Which meant keeping her attraction to Aristos buried deep.

CHAPTER EIGHT

HIS KEY INVESTORS locked down for the game, Aristos turned his attention to the rest of his business he'd been neglecting as he attempted to hold the Akathinian project together.

It was a daunting task. With thirty-three hotels in eleven countries, he relied on his property and country managers to handle issues in his absence and keep things afloat. Luckily, the team he'd handpicked was superior, and by the Thursday before his poker weekend, he'd caught up to a point where things were once again running like a well-oiled machine. His creative strategies for avoiding his attraction to his princess, however, could use some work.

With both of them on their best behavior and Alex immersed in the party planning, he would have thought the undercurrent between them would have faded. Instead it had grown stronger.

If he'd found her undeniably attractive before, Alex in her element, brimming with confidence, was even sexier. It was impossible not to respond to the vibrant, enthusiastic flip side to her vulnerability as she chatted about how the party was coming along at dinner and the ideas she had. It was like watching her potential surface, and it did something funny to his insides.

She was smart, creative and perceptive, her glass-half-full approach to life a fascinating, compelling foil for his jaded view of the world. Which subsequently rendered his list of strategies, his attempts at dry, safe dinner conversation, wholly ineffective. He, a creature who thrived on self-inflicted solitary confinement, looked *forward* to her company at dinner every night.

A buzz sounded from his desk. His gaze flicked to his mobile. *David.*

"Just checking to see if you're still alive," his mentor said drily. "You've gone deep underground."

Which in the past had not always been a good sign. When his darkness caught up with him… He got up to roam to the window, the moon a thin new slice in a dark sky. "Been busy pinning down investors for the game."

"Got everyone you need?"

"Now I have. Dimitri was being elusive."

There was a pause on the other end of the line. "You sure you trust him? I can try to line something else up here."

"I've got it," he said, his tone clipped. He wasn't about to let his mentor, a man who owned half of Las Vegas, rush to his rescue. Especially when David had made it clear he thought he'd pushed it too far this time.

"I appreciate the offer," he added in a more conciliatory tone. "But I'm good. I am looking forward to seeing you, though. Going to ditch those amateur bets you were making last year?"

"Going to get over the need to prove yourself? You've done it a hundred times over, Aristos."

And there it was, David's usual slice of advice delivered in a succinct left hook. He picked up the stress ball sitting on the windowsill and crushed it between his fingers. "Maybe when Akathinia's done."

Maybe when he felt he had the respect due to him that had never quite seemed to come. When his critics finally stopped finding reasons, trumped-up flaws in his visions, to leave him waiting in the wings while his competitors graced the covers of glossy magazines.

David bantered on for a few minutes, then signed off to go to bed. Aristos put the phone down, rested his palms on the sill and looked out at the perfection of a clear Larikos night.

The sense of accomplishment the rush of the week had provided faded in the silence of the darkened room, a bone weariness settling over him. *When are you going to get over trying to prove yourself?*

He was tired of fighting, he acknowledged. Exhausted from attempting to one-up the competition to get to the pinnacle—to be the name on everyone's lips in a fickle entertainment industry that changed on a dime. He thought maybe Akathinia had to be it. *The one.* Wasn't sure how much he had left in him.

He stared out at the clear, bright sky, littered with a sea of stars. What weighed on his mind, ate away at him when he allowed himself time to think, was what he would find when that day came—when he'd exorcised his demons, what he'd find underneath. He suspected it would be an empty shell—that he'd traded his soul for success.

It was why being in perpetual motion was the only way he knew how to operate. Pushing away from the window, he was about to return to his desk to finish up the report he'd been working on when a flash of white caught his eye, picked up by the floodlights on the beach. Alex, who'd stopped working hours ago with most of the details for the party wrapped, stopped under a palm tree, reached into her beach bag and pulled out a blanket. Shaking it out on the sand, she sat down, her eyes on the sky.

The meteor shower was tonight. He'd totally forgotten. In actual fact, despite his sarcasm, he found them fascinating and stunningly beautiful.

Like the woman who sat waiting for the show.

He should finish the report. Instead he found himself shutting off the lights and heading for the beach, his footsteps measured and purposeful. Just like that night in the palace gardens, it was clear to him he should be walking in the opposite direction from the one he was. But he was afraid he'd think too much in his own head, so he walked toward temptation instead.

He'd been resisting her for two weeks. Surely he had this down by now?

Alex looked up as he approached. "There are still front-row seats available."

"You remembered." His gaze touched her tanned, shapely thighs revealed by the modest hem of the shorts she wore, the kind of curves that stopped a man in the street. He didn't need to see more to know they were the perfect toned framework for the fantasies he'd had. Fantasies that involved him ordering her to wrap them around him as he demonstrated what steady-as-they-go Sebastien had clearly not had in his repertoire.

Hot, hard and memorable.

Color darkened her cheekbones. "Your scintillating, well-versed recap of the sight to be seen wouldn't allow me to stay away. I will, however, point out those types of looks are not within our rules."

"True," he agreed, settling himself down beside her on the blanket. "I, however, am in a bit of a mood. You want careful, Princess, you should send me on my way."

She stayed where she was, still as a statue. His excellent peripheral vision caught the big inhale that lifted her chest before she pulled her knees up to it and wrapped her arms around them.

"I thought you'd solved your biggest problem with Dimitri."

He settled himself back on his elbows. "I'm not getting a good vibe from him. I still have to convince him not to bolt."

"What happens if he does?"

"It leaves me one hundred million dollars short of financing. Not to mention the precedent that could set for other investors."

"That must be worrisome. But like you yourself said, you can only control what's within your power."

His mouth twisted. "A little difficult to tell yourself that when you have a half a billion dollars riding on a casino. But I'll give it my best shot, Princess."

She gave him a long look. Sat back on her elbows, mirroring his pose. "It should start soon. It said nine thirty on the web."

A silence fell between them. He studied the push and pull of the sea as it ate up the sand, inching its way forward in a steady, ancient rhythm. *Inescapable, unrelenting.*

Alex was right. He had shored up every weak link within his power. Dimitri was a wild card who played outside the usual rules—he'd known that from the start.

"It's so quiet here," she said after a while.

His gaze flicked to her. "Your village must be quiet. How many people live there?"

"A couple hundred, many of them my mother's family. And yes," she said, a wry note to her voice, "it's sleepy, caught in a past generation. Important announcements are still posted on the *platias* in the village, the fish truck still delivers the catch of the day and the farmers bring the milk to our door."

"How quaint."

"I like it. It's the best way to start my day. Sam, the farmer's son, and I always have the most interesting conversations."

He smiled. He'd bet it was the highlight of Sam's day, too.

"On Sundays we work a half day, let our weekend manager handle things. We have a big dinner with family, family being a loose term that usually encompasses everyone—neighbors, anyone who's around from the neighboring village. It's a big gossip fest, a chance to catch up. Someone handles the grill, someone's playing music, there are kids, dogs everywhere…all a little maniacal. When it's over, my head is usually buzzing so much I'll escape to my favorite little cove to read, center myself, before the week starts."

"It sounds wonderful." A hollow feeling invaded him. His cynical wasteland of an existence couldn't be more different from the reality Alex had lived, from the warmth and community she had been surrounded with. It would be like setting Alice in Wonderland down in the middle of Dante's Inferno…or perhaps Purgatory, he conceded, although he wasn't sure he'd rid himself of all his vices before he'd climbed out.

A throb unfurled low in his gut, wrapping itself around him and squeezing hard. It had never bothered him before, the emptiness of his existence, the connections he'd severed, the absence of affection he'd grown up with. But tonight it did.

A bitter regret assailed him, a sorrow that lingered just beyond the edges—for what he hadn't had, for the things he'd craved so deeply he'd had to let them go before they destroyed him. Guilt. Guilt for what he'd done. Guilt for what he *hadn't* done. Guilt for all of it.

He pinned his gaze on the sea. Fought against the emotion that seemed ever so close to the surface. Alex sat quietly beside him, giving him space in that intuitive way of hers she had. In that way she had of *knowing* him.

If he was pretty sure he'd forgotten how to connect with people—if he'd ever understood the concept—he'd never had that problem with this woman. Their connection had been real from that first night at the ball. Powerful. It had prompted him to reveal parts of himself he'd sworn he never would. If that wasn't enough to make him run, he wasn't sure what would.

Alex absorbed the turbulence of the man sitting beside her. He was clearly working through something in this dark mood he'd announced upon sitting down, as if he wanted to be here and didn't all at the same time.

"You were right," she said quietly, when she'd decided his brooding had gone on long enough. "What you said in the gardens at the palace. I told myself it was enough, my life in Stygos, and it *was* wonderful, I am blessed to have had it. But it was too safe. I needed to leave to find out who I am. I needed to step outside my comfort zone."

His mouth curved. "You've done that, all right. Still feel like it's the right decision?"

"Yes." She pressed her palms to her cheeks, marveling at everything that had happened since that night. "Identifying where I want to put my energy, planning this party, I feel like myself again, only better. Because I know I have all these amazing experiences out there waiting for me."

He blinked, his dark lashes shading his cheeks. "You will be a force to be reckoned with. I have no doubt about it, Princess."

Something unfolded inside her, a warmth, a yearning that was shocking in its intensity. Pressing her lips together, she lowered her gaze, attempting to wrestle her feelings under control. Her eyes slid over the dark purple tattoo half hidden by the sleeve of his T-shirt. Reaching up, she traced it with her fingertips. "What's this? I've seen some of the guards with it."

He pushed his T-shirt higher. "It's a man-of-war. It's the marking my gang members and I carried."

"You brought some of them with you here to Larikos?"

He nodded. "I knew I needed the best in protection for the clientele we would host. Knew I could trust them. Their allegiance is unquestionable, as is their ability to keep a man alive."

A shiver went through her. She traced the intricate detailing of the beautiful design. Done in varying shades of purple and black, it perfectly represented the dangerous creature that had inhabited the seas she'd grown up in, an animal she'd been warned away from as a child. Fascinating, but to be avoided if you knew what was good for you. Like Aristos himself.

She absorbed the corded, impressive muscle beneath her fingertips. It was intoxicating to touch him, to give herself permission to explore his beautiful body for a purely innocent reason. Except she wasn't sure it was so innocent, touching him, not when she lifted her gaze to his and found a banked heat there that made her insides simmer.

She let her fingers fall away from his skin. "What is the significance of the man-of-war?"

"They are deceptively beautiful. Deadly in numbers."

Her lashes arced over her cheeks. "Were you? Deadly?"

He eyed her. "What are you asking me, Princess? If I've ever killed a man?"

"Yes."

"No. My organization, the Men of War as we were known, thought of ourselves as revolutionaries. We were soldiers, taking from the haves to give to the have-nots, reclaiming what society had taken from us. There was a sense of justice to it. It was mostly petty thievery, some armed robberies. There were a few instances where things got out of hand, yes, people got hurt, but those were the hard-core personalities, not the majority."

She stared at him, fascinated. "What was the background of the members? What led them into it?"

"Poverty, violence at home, single-parent families in which the mother was left to cope. The gang provided the bonds we didn't have at home, leadership figures, brother figures…"

"And you?" she asked quietly, her heart in her throat. "What kind of a home did you come from?"

"A broken one. A poor one. My father was a mechanic,

an alcoholic, chronically unfaithful to my mother, often out of work. They fought constantly."

"Was that what drove you out of the house?"

"Partially. I got older, stronger. My father and I would go head-to-head. It was either that or let my rage get the better of me."

"How did they react, your parents, about you joining a gang?"

"My father was furious. He gave me an ultimatum— quit, get back in school or stay away."

"So you chose to stay away?"

"Yes."

"How old were you?"

"Fourteen."

Her chest tightened. *So young. Cast out of his home for reasons that should never have been in the first place.*

"What about your mother? Your brothers and sisters? It must have been difficult to leave them behind."

A silence followed, so long, so pronounced, it made her fear she'd crossed the line, gone too far in her need to know. His reply when it came was low, tight. "My anger was tearing me up. I was afraid of what would happen if I stayed, afraid of what would happen if I left."

The band around her chest tightened. "An impossible decision," she said softly.

"Yes."

"Do you know how they're doing, your family?"

"My mother kicked my father out the year after I joined the gang. She'd had enough. When I sold my first hotel, I went home and bought her a house, made sure she never had to work again. Beyond that, we've had very little contact with each other."

And therein lay the key to so much about this man. Alienated from the family he'd loved, damned if he did, damned if he didn't, he'd cut himself off from feeling, from *allowing* himself to feel because, she suspected, it hurt too much.

She bit the inside of her mouth. "Family is everything, Aristos. Family is the thing you have when everything else is gone. I know you said those ties have been severed, but surely nothing is irreparable?"

"This is."

"But—"

"Angel." The warning in his voice was clear, the glitter in his dark eyes sending a shiver down her spine. "I know you love where you come from. I know you like to idealize that paradise on earth you think it is, but not everyone gets to have that. Sometimes you get hell on earth instead. Sometimes wishing for things you'll never have is too expensive a proposition to keep."

She digested that stunning proclamation, her heart thudding painfully in her chest. She knew the feeling well. She'd spent her life wishing for a father who loved her, only to be served up with reality instead. But Aristos was talking about his *life*. About the love and care he'd never had, not until David Tennyson had picked him up off the street at sixteen, perhaps too late to ever heal the wounds inside him.

If she'd been living her life on the pages of a book, Aristos had been living his in a bitter existence no one should ever have to experience. Making choices no one should ever have to make.

Her head was still spinning when Aristos pointed at the sky. "There's one."

She looked up, watching a bright ball shoot horizontally across the inky black sky, a trail of light flaring behind it. Not far behind was another, then another, until the heavens were a stunning display of bursts, streams and flutters of light.

Spellbound, she drank it in. On and on it went in a symphony of color. When a particularly jaw-dropping explosion scorched the sky, she reached for Aristos's arm to point it out to him, but her hand landed on his thigh instead.

Tight, hard muscle coiled beneath her palm; his heat bleeding into her. An electrical current vibrated from where she touched him up through her arm to encompass her entire body. It tore her gaze from the sky and planted it solidly on that of the man beside her. If her heart hadn't been firmly secured in her chest, it would surely have jumped right out of it at the look on his face.

Jaw set, expression predatory, the fire in his eyes made the blood pound in her veins.

The world could have exploded around her in that moment and it wouldn't have stopped her from drifting toward him, toward the imminent collision she knew would be as explosive as the ones happening in the sky above. Eyes darkening with an emotion she couldn't read, Aristos pressed a palm to her chest, stopping her before she got there.

"*No*, angel."

Her brain didn't immediately compute. She stared at him, confused. He dropped his hands to her waist and rose, lifting her along with him and setting her down on her feet in the sand. Retrieving the blanket, he shook it out, threw it over his arm and propelled her toward the Great House, a hand at the small of her back.

Up the stairs they went, the silence surrounding them deafening. Humiliation heated her cheeks, dragged her every step. When they reached the door to her bedroom, she turned to look at him, leaning back against the frame. "Aristos—"

"Alex." He cut her off with a clipped voice. "That would not have been wise, and you know it."

She brought her back teeth together, corralling her emotions. "You're right," she bit out. "There I go again, throwing myself at you. My deepest apologies…"

Turning, she reached for the door handle. Aristos's fingers clamped around her biceps and spun her to face him. "Alex—"

"Forget it," she snapped furiously. "Let me go."

He backed her up against the wall instead, his palms flattening on either side of her. "Princess," he murmured huskily, pressing his forehead against hers, "I am not rejecting you, I am choosing *sanity*."

Wasn't it the same thing? She sucked in air, attempting to find some of that particular attribute because he was right. Perfectly right. This shouldn't be happening. Except wrong, because she didn't give a flip about sanity. She wanted *this*.

A second passed, two, three maybe, their heat spilling into each other. His mouth was a fraction from hers, so close she was breathing his air. His hard thighs, pressed against hers, broadcasted his arousal.

The oath he uttered then as he levered himself back to stare at her made her stomach clench. "I don't know what I'm doing with you anymore," he rasped, his gaze raking hers. "And tonight is not the night to figure it out. Trust me."

Cool air drifted over her as he stepped back, turned and walked down the hall to his room. Pulse racing, blood pounding in her ears, she watched him go, waiting for her knees to assure her they would function before she pivoted, reached for the doorknob and let herself in the room.

Would her mistakes with that man never end?

CHAPTER NINE

A PICTURE-PERFECT LARIKOS night had presented itself for Galina Smirnov's birthday party, at which the jazz legend Nina Karvelas would sing in public for the first time in over five years.

A blood-orange sky streaked with fingers of yellow marked the occasion, drawing a dressed and ready-to-go Alex out onto the terrace to drink it in as the day sank slowly into night as only a Mediterranean evening could, with its intoxicating blend of vivid colors that stoked the senses.

A flock of butterflies traced a looping path through her stomach. She'd double-, triple-checked that every detail was in place, and still she felt nervous. She wanted it to be perfect for Aristos. Perfect for Nina, with whom she'd met earlier in the day to discuss her charity, another reason for the overabundance of adrenaline running through her veins. It seemed a perfect fit. If Nik approved the choice, she would be off and running.

The butterflies in her stomach intensified. Now if only the tension between her and Aristos could be resolved. He hadn't spoken to her since he'd left her at her door two days before with that cryptic line.

I don't know what I'm doing with you anymore.

What did that even mean? He was conflicted, to be sure. About her, about his feelings for her. He was charged with protecting her, yes, but she suspected his walking away had more to do with how much he'd revealed to her...

the intimate conversation they'd shared...the connection between them neither could seem to control.

What he'd shared with her on the beach that night had been heartbreaking, had followed her around ever since. Had changed *everything*. She could no longer label him a heartless philanderer. Instead she had discovered a complex, wounded man behind those walls he liked to build, a man who'd never been given the tools to connect or love.

She felt empathy for him, yes, but also something far more dangerous: the belief that whatever was happening between them was real, different. That *she* was different to him.

What she'd felt that night when he'd stood there outside her door fighting his emotions hadn't changed. She wanted to be with him, to know that kind of passion. Of all the jumps she'd taken, this might be the biggest, most dangerous, because it involved her heart. Because if they explored what they had, Aristos might break it.

But wasn't that what her new life was all about? Taking the risks she'd always avoided?

Her watch told her it was time to make her way down to the beach. Stepping her feet into crystal-studded flip-flops, a prerequisite for the sandy white beach, she joined the staff as the first guests began to arrive.

The hiss and crackle of the roaring bonfire that licked almost six feet into the air was the star attraction, surrounded by the sultry sounds of Nina's jazz band. Sleek-looking serving staff handed out vibrantly hued cosmopolitans, Galina's favorite cocktail, to inspire a celebratory mood.

She stood surveying the scene as the beach filled up, a satisfied smile curving her lips. Not only were the Smirnovs and their guests here, but every single one of Aristos's poker players was, too, clearly anticipating the show. As long as nothing went wrong with the acoustics, which weren't a given with the tricky winds of late, the evening would be a smash success.

Her gaze shifted to Aristos, who stood speaking to the guests of honor, Dimitri Smirnov and his wife, Galina. Galina was as lovely as her superior hostess reputation had suggested; her husband, on the other hand, was another story. His reputation preceded him; first impressions hadn't improved it. He struck her as cocky, not entirely transparent and full of himself.

Aristos, meanwhile, had a very different impact on her. Elegant in a silver-gray shirt and black pants, his short-cropped dark hair pushed back from his face in a ruffled, spiky look, he oozed intensity. He reminded her of the fire dancing and crackling behind him: beautiful, imminently combustible, undeniably dangerous, a dozen layers deep, each one a darker, more complex version than the last.

Her stomach dipped, a wave of heat shimmering through her. What would it be like to have that single-minded intensity focused on you and you alone? She'd had a taste of it. It had been enough to convince her it would be worth every heart-stopping second.

He looked at her then, before she had a chance to wipe the evidence from her face. Moved that intense gaze over the sophisticated French twist she'd engineered, down over her face, where ebony eyes tangled with blue for a long, suspended moment, then over the sleek black dress that skimmed her curves, cataloging every inch, every centimeter as he went.

She sucked in a breath, heat bleeding into her skin as if he'd physically touched her. It shook her in her shoes, vibrating every inch of her skin, as if for a moment, he'd forgotten to marshal his defenses, that impressive control of his, and all she could see was the truth. The hunger.

He didn't want to want her, but he did.

He moved his gaze back to her face. Tension thickened

the air between them. Held her frozen. Then rationality, in precious little quantity of late, thankfully kicked in. She wasn't letting Mr. Hot-and-Cold take her on an emotional roller-coaster ride tonight. Not when so much was riding on the success of this party, for her and for him.

Turning her back on his stare, she made her way into the crowd.

Aristos absorbed the princess's turned back with a blink and then another, noting, of course, her amazing behind in the formfitting black dress, because she had the best one he'd ever seen.

Was that just a kiss-off look? He thought it might have been... He'd never actually had one to compare it to.

It stirred an animalistic desire to wipe it off her face even though he knew exactly why she'd directed it at him. That he deserved it. This time he *had* been running for the hills. Sharing your life story with a woman you were clearly developing feelings for did that to a man. Well, that, and he'd been completely focused on the game, on clearing the decks so he could devote his attention to his investors tonight.

It ate away at him, that look. Festered as he found himself watching Alex rather than Nina's performance, as spectacular as it was, wondering what he was doing with her. He'd walked away from her the other night because Nik had told him in no uncertain terms that she wasn't to be his—that hadn't changed. Yet every time he came within a foot of her, those good intentions flew out the window, clouded by a complex set of emotions and lust he couldn't seem to make head nor tail of.

The lust he could handle, decipher. The other feelings Alex aroused in him, not so much. That he had cared for her from the start was clear if you shone a light on his behavior. What he felt for her now was more complex.

She was getting under his skin, making him feel things, question things, *want* things he couldn't have. He couldn't turn her off like a switch as he did with his other women.

That was the heart of the issue. The source of his problem. But he thought maybe he could have handled it better.

He pulled her aside after the performance as the guests mingled. Alex gave him another of those cool looks.

"Everything okay?" he asked deliberately.

"Kala." She lifted her chin. "Everything's going perfectly. Don't you think it's perfect?"

"Perfect," he agreed. "I came over to say thank you."

"It's the least I can do." The words rolled off her tongue in swift, robotic fashion, stirring the antagonism roiling his insides. "Galina would like to watch the game," she said. "Can I watch it with her?"

"Women are distracting."

"Then why do you have the two beautiful waitresses? I saw them earlier."

"Because they're meant to distract, entertain the men. You are not."

Her mouth firmed. "I will stay in the background. Firmly in the background. Let me come."

His better judgment told him no, but this was Alex and her big blue eyes he was up against—an unfair battle.

"In the background," he underscored. "You blend in with the paint."

The high rollers' room glittered with opulence: Brazilian-wood floors shone underfoot, the marble showpiece of a bar was lined with hundreds of colorfully hued bottles and the arched, elegant glass doors that lined the wall to the terrace were magnificent, cut crystal shimmering in the muted lighting.

The air was tense, thick, the players bent in concentration over their cards. Aristos, Dimitri, the sultan she'd met earlier, a senator from New York and six other men sat around the table in the center of the room. Whiskey glasses littered the surface of the table, ties lay discarded on the backs of chairs and the aroma of cigars lingered alongside the overpowering scent of competition.

One of the beautiful blonde waitresses clad in a black dress far sexier than Alex's ushered her and Galina around the edge of the room to the bar.

"Is it always this quiet?" Alex whispered, sliding onto a stool.

"No. Tense game."

"Who's winning?"

"Kako, then the sultan, then Aristos."

Kako, the pro who had won last year... "How much is on the table?"

"Eight million."

Thee mou. She almost swallowed her tongue.

Ensuring Galina had a drink in her hand, she procured a glass of champagne from the bartender. Off duty now and able to relax, a victorious rush moved through her. Nina's performance had gone perfectly, Galina was ecstatic and Aristos had spent much of the party with the Smirnovs.

For the first time in weeks, she didn't feel helpless. Didn't feel carried along by forces far greater than herself. She had proven she could execute a charity event for VIPs and make it a success. It gave her the confidence that when she resumed her real life as a princess and her upcoming work with Nina, she could do good things in the world, that she could own the role.

It sank into her bones, that heady feeling, as she watched the game. Aristos, sleeves rolled up to his elbows, corded, muscular forearms exposed, took the round, pulling the pile of chips toward the stacks he had in front of him. Triumph glittered in his ebony eyes as he leaned back and drained his scotch.

The dealer set out the next hand. The senator stretched while he did, noticing her and Galina sitting at the bar and smiling a greeting. She returned the smile, keeping it brief. Blending with the paint, that's what she was doing.

But the sultan, who already had two wives although he'd been flirting outrageously with Alex at the party, noticed her, too. His overt stare caused a ripple effect around the table as the rest of the men turned to look.

Aristos narrowed his gaze on her. Turning on her stool, she devoted her attention to her glass of champagne and Galina.

The next round began. The sultan took it, Kako the one after that, then Aristos in a nail-biting hand that stretched the tension in the room to a breaking point.

The sultan looked most displeased. Kako gave a shake of his head, requested a break and headed out of the room. The tension broke then, the table dissolving into good-natured ribbing, one of the professional players flirting heavily with the blond-haired waitress as she served him a drink. The sultan remained silent, pouty, if a man could be described as that, sitting back in his chair, arms crossed over his chest.

"Maybe," he announced, setting his gaze on Alex, "we should up the ante for the next round."

Galina sucked in a breath. Alex sat up straight. Aristos followed the sultan's gaze to her, eyes narrowing. "What are you proposing?"

"Her," said the sultan, nodding at Alex. "Winner of the next round."

Her stomach fell to the floor. A silence filled the room. Aristos sat back in his chair, the expression on his face unchanged. "We don't play by those rules here. You know that."

They did somewhere else?

"Maybe we need to shake things up a bit."

"Not happening," Aristos drawled.

"Why?" The sultan gave him a belligerent look. "Is she yours?"

One of the pro players made a choked sound. The senator's eyes went round. The icy expression that passed across Aristos's face sent a chill down her spine. "Yes, as a matter of fact," he drawled, "she is."

The sultan held up his hands, a rueful twist to his lips. "Fair enough. You have to admit, Nicolades, you weren't making it very obvious."

Because she wasn't his. Because this was insane.

Aristos pushed his chair back, stood and walked over to where she sat at the bar. His spicy cologne infiltrated her senses as he barked a request to the bartender for a scotch, his eyes never leaving hers. He waited until the drink was poured, wrapped his fingers around the tumbler, clamped a hand around her upper arm and pulled her off the stool.

Her breath caught in her throat. Too intimidated to protest, she allowed him to guide her out onto the terrace while the whole table watched.

She waited until they were out of sight and earshot of the others before she pulled her arm out of his grip. "Enough of your caveman tactics, thank you."

He leaned against the railing and knocked back a gulp of scotch. Fixed his gaze on her. "I told you this was a bad idea. These men are a different breed, Alex."

As was he. It thrilled and intimidated her all at the same time.

"Did he mean it?"

"Undoubtedly."

"Did *you*?"

His eyes flashed. "Alex," he growled. "There are millions of dollars on that table. We are not doing this now."

"I know," she said, moving closer to him. "But I'd like to know the answer to the question."

"You can't be mine," he rasped, his gaze tracking her. "You want my list again? You are off-limits. I don't do relationships. My affairs are short-lived, transactional entities where everyone knows the score."

"What if I did, want that, I mean? To explore what's between us."

His gaze narrowed. "You are a princess. Third in line to the throne in case you'd forgotten…whom I'm supposed to be protecting."

"There's no threat here," she derided. "The only thing you're protecting me from is you."

"Exactly."

Her pulse gave a tremendous flutter, then took off at a full gallop. "And if I weren't…off-limits to you?"

"There's no point in discussing it, because you are."

She fixed her gaze on his. "I saw your face tonight. That night on the beach…"

"*Christos*, Alex." He raked a hand through his hair. "You've just walked right out of *Alice in Wonderland*. I am not the man for you. I don't do flowers and chocolate."

"I'm not asking for that…for a relationship. I want to explore what's between us. What that kind of passion feels like. That's all."

"That's all?" He stared at her. Set his glass down on the railing with a deliberate movement. "Are you trying to wreck my head?"

She shook hers. "I'm merely suggesting, as you yourself said, that we do what we both want."

"No."

She eyed him, frustration coursing through her. "You know what I think? I think you're all talk, Aristos. I think you throw these challenges at me, these scenarios of what it would be like between us, because you know I won't act on them. It's *safe*. And when I do, you run." She lifted her chin. "I think you're scared. I think you have no idea what will happen between us if we actually face up to this attraction."

"Oh, I know," he rasped, eyes flashing. "We would be incendiary together, angel. We would blow the doors off my bedroom, and this would turn into an even bigger mess than it already is."

"Or it would solve our problem… We could address it and put it behind us. No one would have to know."

A long moment passed. "Just so we're clear," he ventured in a silky voice, "you're suggesting we have an affair? Confined to this island?"

"Yes."

"No."

"Why?" She tugged her bottom lip between her teeth. "You said I was bored with Sebastien and you were right. You told me to define my life, to go after what I want. Here I am, going after what I want."

He uttered one of the filthiest curse words in the Greek language. She winced, absorbing his fury. Taking her by the hand, he marched her back into the room, issued an "all non-players out" command directed at Galina, then propelled her out of the room past a sea of amused faces, a palm at her back.

Across the beach they went, up the stairs to the Great House and down the hall to her room. Her heart was pounding like a freight train by the time he opened her door and pushed her inside.

"You," he said, "will stay here. You will not come anywhere near the game. I will deal with you when it's done." He pinned his gaze on her face. "Understood?"

"Yes." She tucked a stray chunk of hair behind her ear. "But you could tell me—"

Thud. The door slammed behind him.

*　*　*

Aristos stopped drinking after that. It had only been his second scotch; he'd been pacing himself, as had all the men, except the sultan, of course, who didn't drink. But any amount of alcohol in his brain after what Alex had just done to him was too much.

He set his second-to-last hand down, a good one. Sat back in his chair as Kako grimaced.

No one would have to know. It would just be between the two of them… Theos. A synapse in his brain snapped. *You told me to define my life, to go after what I want. Here I am, going after what I want.*

He wiped a hand across his brow. He had created this monster. This was his mess to deal with. The question was, what was he going to do about it?

He allocated half his attention to the sultan's hand, the rest of it sitting firmly back in that room at the Great House with the woman he now conceded he wanted more than he'd ever wanted one in his life. The same one who had just offered herself up to him for a no-holds-barred, private affair.

She was right, he acknowledged as the sultan set down a full house, a better hand than his. What he'd been offering were excuses, excuses that had been protecting him from her. From the lust he felt for her. From whatever else he felt for her that he refused to examine. Except for the king and his casino contract, of course. That was a very real deterrent to taking what she was offering.

But if he and the princess kept this between them, no one would have to know.

Kako set down a brilliant hand. Aristos scowled and took a sip of water. Examined the last point to be considered. He was afraid he would hurt Alex. Afraid he had no idea how to play this game when his feelings were involved. When it wasn't just sex. He knew he couldn't give her what she needed in the long run, but she'd said she wasn't looking for a relationship.

Could she handle an affair, however, that ended when his interest waned? Which it would once he'd solved her mysteries. It was always that way with him: the allure of a woman fading when she was no longer an enigma to him. The thrill of the chase in its most classic format.

If he agreed to what Alex was proposing, she had to be clear on the rules. The boundaries. Truthfully, he was starting to think a controlled experiment, like allowing a fire to burn under carefully monitored circumstances, was the only way forward for them. To burn this attraction out completely.

She was affecting his head. Impeding his ability to focus at the most critical time in his career. He couldn't have it.

An image of himself on his knees, his hands on Alex's delectable body, tightened his fingers around the tumbler. Those sexy moans she made when she couldn't help herself…

An impatient sigh broke through his fantasy. "I know she's hot," said Kako. "Hell, I'd be long gone by now, but could you please," he said, waving his hand at him, "take a card or pass so we can find a winner?"

Ignoring the pro's gibe, Aristos lifted his hand and requested two more cards. It wasn't enough.

The final result: Kako first, Aristos second, the sultan third.

He offered Kako his congratulations, his own mood rather surly now as he watched his millions piled in front of the pro. He intended to exact retribution for the result, in only the most pleasurable way, of course.

CHAPTER TEN

ALEX STOOD, FOREARMS resting on the terrace railing, contemplating the floodlit beach as the clock ticked past 2:00 a.m. The lap of the waves against the shore and the persistent song of the cicadas were the only sounds that filled the air, not enough to drown out the pounding in her ears.

She'd seen some of the players disperse along the beach toward their private villas, which meant Aristos would be done soon. Adrenaline coursed through her, tightening her skin, quickening her heart. Had Aristos meant tonight when the game was over they would settle this between them? Or perhaps when all the players had gone home? Since that wouldn't be until tomorrow afternoon, she thought it might actually kill her. She'd stayed dressed just in case.

A knock on her door ten minutes later had her jumping out of her skin. Waiting for it, anticipating it, she froze, all of a sudden utterly unsure of what she was doing.

It came again. Pulling herself out of her suspended state, she walked inside, crossed to the door and released the bolt. Aristos, tie slung over his shoulder, a bottle of champagne in his hand, stood leaning against the wall.

Apparently the intensity he'd been wearing hadn't ended with the game. The look he sliced over her was pure predator. It held her feet rooted to the ground, eyes fixed on his.

"You going to let me in, Princess?" His low drawl raked over her sensitized skin. "A discreet affair might not entail me standing in the hallway with a bottle of champagne in my hand."

Her heart skipped a beat. Is that what they were having?

She stepped back before it appeared she'd lost all her brain cells. Aristos straightened away from the doorway and moved inside, leaving behind a waft of that delicious spicy scent he wore.

She closed the door.

"Lock it." His evenly delivered command told her exactly how this was going to go. Made her stomach cave to the floor. She twisted the bolt shut with hands that weren't quite steady. Turned around to find him uncorking the bottle.

"Who won?"

"Kako."

"Oh." She pushed a chunk of hair out of her face. "I'm sorry about that."

"You should be." A *pop* as he worked the cork free made her jump. "I was in it up until those last couple of hands. You destroyed my concentration."

She searched his face for some sign he was joking, but there was none. Just that same intensity, clawing its way across her nerves.

"I really am sorry. I had no idea the sultan would be so…outrageous."

"I told you that game is no place for a woman."

"Do they actually bet *women* in these games? Isn't that against some sort of law?"

"There are no rules for some of these men. The sultan, Dimitri, they live in a whole other universe. It would never happen in one of my games, though, and they know it."

She shivered. "I didn't like him—Dimitri. Doesn't his background bother you? His unethical business practices? The rumors of far worse?"

"They are rumors, *paidi mou*. Exactly that. Show me a rich man who doesn't have shadows."

The casual endearment stirred the anticipation churning her insides. Her stomach lurched as he moved closer, the bottle of champagne in his hand. Close enough she could feel the heat of his big body. It moved through her, stung her with its all-enveloping warmth.

He raked his gaze over her face. "So here's the thing. I think you're right we need to tackle this problem of ours. Face up to this attraction we share. An affair would do that. But I need to know you can handle this, Alex. That you're not jumping in with this newfound confidence of yours only to realize it's been a big mistake."

She shook her head, heart battering her ribs so hard she thought it might break free. "I won't. I know what I want."

He lifted a hand and brushed the back of his knuckles over her heated cheek. "This starts and ends here. Nobody gets hurt…"

She nodded. He was protecting her with his caveats, but he was also protecting himself.

Aristos's eyes darkened, the only outward sign he had acknowledged the decision they'd just made. He took a long swig of the champagne straight from the bottle, then passed it to her. She closed her fingers around the ice-cold glass. "Not very princess-like."

"Nothing about tonight is going to be very princess-like," he murmured, snaking an arm around her waist and pulling her into all that solid heat. "Except me granting your every wish… I might be persuaded to do that as long as I have leeway to make some demands of my own."

She didn't dare even wonder what those demands would be. Had enough on her plate at the moment, quite frankly. She lifted the bottle to her mouth and took a sip of the dry, fruity vintage. It tasted intoxicating, heady. When Aristos cupped the back of her head and took her mouth in a kiss that wasted no time in getting to the point, her head spun.

His tongue dipped inside her mouth, sliding against hers in a leisurely exploration. His throaty murmur of approval skated across her cheek. "I love champagne on you. You taste so sweet, *moro mou.*"

Bringing the bottle to her mouth, he fed her another swallow. Dipped his head to consume it with her. She had never experienced anything so erotic, so intimate. He fed her a few more sips in between those sweet, hot kisses until she had melted against him, completely under his spell.

He captured her bottom lip in his and bit lightly, the sharp reprimand catching her off guard. "This mouth," he growled, "does something to me... Every time I tell myself I have to stay away, I can't. You are wrecking my head, Princess."

Her stomach folded in on itself. She leaned back, drinking him in. "I love kissing you. It's almost...spiritual."

His gaze darkened. Setting the bottle down, he took the weight of her hips in his palms, dragging her closer. "Do it again," he instructed, covering her mouth with his. She did, kissing him back, exploring his beautiful mouth with teasing nibbles of her own. He tightened his hands around her hips and pulled her into him, settling her against the erection that strained his trousers. She gasped at the size of him.

"That's right, angel...your kisses do that to me."

That they did blew her mind. A light-headed feeling descended over her as Aristos buried his mouth in her throat, seeking out her pleasure points while his palms held her hips in place for the sensual, intoxicating slide of his thick length against her core.

When Sebastien had kissed her, it'd been pleasant. *These* kisses were turning her insides to molten heat. Making her forget she'd ever had nerves.

A low moan escaped her throat.

"You want more?"

"Yes."

He slid his hands down the back of her thighs and pushed her dress up. Easing his knee between her legs, his hard muscle found her throbbing core. The friction, his purposeful movements, the heat of his gaze as he watched her, sent bolts of pleasure rippling through her. The aching flesh between her thighs grew wet, supple, his to command.

"Aristos."

"You like that, angel?"

"Yes."

The helpless, raspy note to her voice sounded foreign to her. She didn't know what she wanted. Needed. She knew only that she wanted more.

He dropped to his knees. Her spinning head attempted to determine what he was doing. Closing his hands around her thighs, he nudged them apart, a look of such wicked intent on his face, her breath stopped in her throat.

"Aristos—"

He looked up at her. Read the hesitation in her face. "You've never had a man do this for you?"

"No." She hadn't had a man do anything to her beyond kissing her. But she thought the timing was all off to tell him that now.

"Consider it another of your firsts," he said huskily. "I'm pretty sure it was the thought of you, spread out for me like this, that lost me the game."

Theos. "It's too—"

"Angel," he said firmly, "trust me."

She did. Had trusted him from the beginning. She relaxed her thighs, giving way to the firm pressure of his palms. His hands pushed her dress up to her waist. The look on his face when he discovered the wispy black thong she wore made her stomach dissolve. "You kill me," he murmured. "You are so beautiful, Princess. I want to *know* you. Every part of you."

Any further qualms she might have had dissolved with those words. His thumbs slid under the sides of the thong to ease it off her hips. She stepped out of it for him, blood pounding in her ears. She closed her eyes after that as he parted her thighs wider. One hand on her hip, he slid a finger down the length of her most intimate flesh. She jerked against his touch, but he held her in place. "So aroused," he murmured, repeating the caress with a more insistent movement. "As hot for me as I am for you."

When he parted her with gentle fingers, she thought her heart might jump through her chest. His breath was a warm, heady caress against her skin, announcing his intention to touch her just before his tongue made a leisurely foray where his fingers had been. She bucked into his hold. He held her firmly, sliding his tongue over her again, finding the tight bundle of nerves at the heart of her this time. A white-hot pleasure exploded through her.

She buried her fingers in his hair as he nudged her nub with his tongue. Over her, against her, he moved, increasing his rhythm until the almost-impossible sensitivity dissolved on a hot rush of sensation.

"This is how I wanted you," he rasped, lifting his mouth from her flesh. "Completely at my mercy. Begging for the pleasure you know I can give you."

She was too far gone to respond. Her eyes flew open as Aristos slid one of his long, elegant fingers inside her.

"Easy, angel," he murmured. "I've got you. I promise."

Her hands clenched his hair as he moved his finger in and out of her in an exquisite torture that stoked the fire inside her higher. When he added another, filling her completely, she started sliding down a starry path of no return.

She moaned his name, the desperate edge to her voice shocking her. Keeping up that delicious rhythm with his fingers, he brought his tongue back to the tight nub at the heart of her. "That's it," he murmured against her flesh. "Let go, angel."

She arched her hips against his mouth. He took her apart with a deliberate flick of his tongue that pushed the white-hot pleasure to its peak. Her orgasm racked her, blinding her, her legs giving way beneath her.

He held her up as, spent, shaken, she recovered, waves of aftershocks shivering through her. When the earth had righted itself, he slid an arm under her knees and picked her up, carrying her to the bed.

Setting her down beside it, he reached for the buttons of his shirt. Rapidly, his gaze on her the whole time, he undid it and dragged it off, then reached for the button of his pants. Her heart jumped into her throat as he pushed them off his hips and stepped out of them. He was all solid, powerful muscle. Vastly intimidating. Not to mention the part of him that was fully aroused beneath his black boxers. It made her mouth go dry. Excessively dry.

She headed straight for the champagne bottle, picked it up and took a healthy swallow.

He sat down on the bed. "Nerves, angel?"

He had no idea. He really didn't.

She took another sip of the champagne.

"Bring it over," he suggested.

"No," she said, taking another drink, "I'm good."

Aristos had no problem waiting her out. He might be way past gone where Alex was concerned, but he intended to take his time with her. Play to her inexperience this time around. Later was another story...

When she eventually set the bottle down and walked back over to him, he took her in from head to toe, watching a flush work its way across her beautiful olive skin as he did. "Take the dress off, Princess."

She blinked. Chewed on her bottom lip. "I need help with the zipper."

He set his hands on her hips and turned her around. Reaching for the zipper, he slid it down to where it ended at the beginning of her delectable bottom. Snagging an arm around her waist, he pulled her against him, pressing his mouth to the delicate column of her spine. A shiver went through her. He moved his hands up to cup her breasts. She arched against him, seeking his touch.

Her responsiveness made the blood fire in his veins. "Take it off," he ordered throatily.

She lifted her hands and pushed the dress off her shoulders. It fell to her hips and caught on the curve of her bottom. Bending, she slid it past her hips to the floor, stepped out of it and kicked it to the side. When she turned around, he knew he'd never seen anything so perfect. She was petite with a Venus-like voluptuousness that was all woman.

He wondered if that was why he needed to possess her so badly. The dominant side of him. The need to protect, to claim what was his. And yet, he reminded himself, frowning past that errant thinking, she would never be his. This was a fling to put their explosive chemistry to rest.

He caught her hand in his and pulled her onto his lap. A tinge of apprehension still lingered in her blue eyes. He covered her mouth with his and kissed her until she was soft beneath his hands, played with the erect points of her nipples with his thumbs until she let out a low moan.

Depositing her on the bed, she landed in a cloud of cream-colored silk. Riffling through his pants, he found the condoms he'd stashed there. Fishing one out, he threw it on the bedside table, slid his fingers under the waistband of his boxers and pushed them off.

Alex's eyes were riveted to the proud thrust of his manhood. Ripping open the package, he slid the condom on, happy to give her a show. When he'd sheathed himself, he joined her on the bed. "This is where you get to tell me how you like it, Princess. Your choice."

Her eyes widened. "It—it doesn't matter. Just…slow, you know."

She was damn lucky he had some self-control left. *Barely.* "Maybe you don't know? Soukis was that tame?"

Her delicate throat convulsed. "I *don't* know. How I like it, I mean…"

Something twisted inside him. "No worries," he murmured, moving over her and caging her with his thighs. "I know how I want you. Underneath me. Wrapped around me, angel, so I can watch your face while I give you everything I have."

Her eyes were huge, sparkling sapphires. Bending his head, he took one of her perfect breasts in his mouth. Applied enough pressure to make her writhe beneath him. She thrust her fingers in his hair and hung on. Devoting the same attention to her other nipple, he slid his hand over her flat stomach, dipped into her warmth and found her wet and ready for him.

His control on shaky ground, he nudged her thighs apart. Guiding one of her legs around his waist, he lifted her bottom with his palm and slid his throbbing flesh against her slick opening. Alex closed her eyes, her fingers catching hold of the silk beneath her. Slowly, deliberately, he caressed her. Waited for the signal she was ready.

"Aristos." His name left her lips on a sigh. Sinking his fingers into the soft flesh of her bottom, he eased himself into her tight, hot body. She was small, petite here, too. He gritted his teeth and took it slowly, allowing her body to soften around his before he continued. The leg Alex had wrapped around his waist tightened, urged him closer. He sank deeper inside her, her snug body heaven and torture all at the same time.

"Okay, angel?"

She nodded, the hazy pleasure in her eyes inflaming his senses. Gripping her buttocks, he surged forward, filling her with all of him. Flinched at the resistance he encountered. His brain struggled to compute. Had it been physical? Mental? The shock spreading across her face, the different tightening of her body around his, the sudden easing now that she'd accommodated him, made it seem as if—

He froze. Surveyed the tension on her face.

"Alex," he said in a dangerously quiet voice, making those blue eyes flutter open. "Tell me you aren't what I think you are."

She bit her lip. He cursed.

Her fingers closed around his forearm. "I wanted it to be you. I made this choice, Aristos."

"And you didn't think to tell me?"

"I should have." She tightened her leg around him, holding him to her. "It's done now. *Parakalo*—I want this. I want *you*."

She was right. The damage was done. It was all his stunned brain could process.

"Please," she said again. "This is what I want."

It was the vulnerability, the hot desire in her gaze that did him in. The knowledge that if he was going to hell, which he surely was now, he was going to enjoy himself while he was doing it. He was going to make her first time the best experience it could be.

Palming her buttock, he began stroking inside her. Her natural eroticism, her passionate response as she lifted her hips to meet his thrusts, stoked the flame inside him back to life. Deepening his strokes, he brought his mouth down on hers and drank from her sweetness. Swallowed her low moans of pleasure.

"You like me inside you? How does it feel to have all of me?"

"Good. *So good.*" She dug her fingernails into his back. "Don't stop. Please don't stop."

There was no way he could now. There was no resistance left in him as he drove himself into her soft, willing body. *Spiritual,* she'd called it. He thought it particularly apt as he buried his mouth in her throat and tasted her racing pulse. Kissing Alex had been one thing. Possessing her another thing entirely. He had the feeling nothing else would satisfy him after this. That she would be imprinted on his brain, ruining him for anything less than what she was.

The tension in his body built to unsustainable levels. Lifting his mouth from hers, he filled his palms with her hips, angling her so he could find that pleasure point deep inside her that could give her an even more intense release than before. He saw it in her eyes, the way the blue turned deep indigo, that she felt it, too.

"Right there," he murmured huskily, stroking that spot again and again with deep, hard thrusts. "Feel me right there."

She started to tremble beneath him. He closed his mouth over hers as she came apart, her moan of pleasure raking through him, completing him in a way he'd never experienced before. It spurred his own violent release. Uttering a hoarse cry, he drove into her sweetness, slaking the lust that had been consuming him for weeks.

A thick silence filled the room as they lay spent, catching their breath. Shifting his weight off Alex, he went into the bathroom and cleaned himself up. When he returned, she was sitting up on the bed, her dark hair in wild disarray, blue eyes wary. "Are you angry?"

"Yes." He raked a hand through his hair. "You should have told me. *Diavole*, Alex, I just took your virginity."

"So?"

"So how does that happen in this day and age? You are twenty-five."

She lifted a shoulder. "I told you. There wasn't much of a chance to meet anyone in Stygos. Sebastien was my only serious boyfriend."

"And he never got you into bed?"

"That's why he asked me to marry him. Because I wouldn't."

She might have been worth it. He shook off that rather insane thought. "So you blithely decided to toss it all away tonight? Just for the hell of it?"

"You know it wasn't like that."

He didn't know anything anymore. Not one damn thing.

"Aristos," she said quietly. "This changes nothing. I'm an adult. I made a decision."

"A decision you didn't consult me about. A decision that has repercussions."

She frowned. "What repercussions?"

He didn't know that, either. Biting out a curse, he gathered his clothes from the floor and threw them on. Alex watched him from the bed, a frozen look on her face. But this time, *this* time, he wasn't going there. He needed to go find his common sense instead.

"Get some sleep. I have guests to see off tomorrow."

"Aristos—"

He left without looking at her. Before temptation led him astray yet again.

CHAPTER ELEVEN

ALEX WOKE WITH a pounding headache, sunshine from another glorious Larikos day streaming in through blinds she'd forgotten to draw. But it wasn't just her head that hurt. She was sore in places that made her cheeks heat.

Burrowing her aching head in the pillow, images from the evening before came at her fast and hard. Her night with Aristos had been hot, tender and passionate, had surpassed any expectations she'd had. Reading about that type of passion on a page and experiencing such heart-stopping intimacy were two entirely different things.

She felt different, changed, more of a woman in every way, as if the universe had opened up yet another facet of itself for her to explore. She didn't regret for one second giving her virginity to Aristos, but apparently he did.

Her head gave another vicious throb. Cradling it in her palm, she closed her eyes. The way he'd vacated her room with the speed of a hotel guest short of funds took the edge off her glow. Killed it dead. Spoiled what should have been perfect.

So she'd been a virgin. What was the big deal? It hadn't seemed to throw off what had surely been an extremely sensual encounter. Or maybe it had? Maybe it had turned Aristos off completely. Maybe she'd disappointed him with her inexperience. Maybe he'd just done a good job of hiding it.

Perhaps it hadn't been as spiritual as she'd felt it to be at all.

Ugh. Opening her eyes, she maneuvered herself into a sitting position. She wasn't going to be *that* girl. Not when she'd promised herself no regrets.

Untangling herself from the silk sheets, she padded to the bathroom, rooted through her toiletry bag and unearthed some aspirin. Downing them with a swig of water, she told herself Aristos's running had more to do with him being Aristos. Because he was a commitment-phobe and she had been a virgin. A deadly creature.

She dressed and went for breakfast on the main terrace, thinking perhaps it would help her head, but when the man in question strode into the dining room with Dimitri Smirnov, offered her a curt nod, then ignored her completely, her stomach shriveled up into a ball unsuitable for the consumption of food.

She gave up and left. Her head finally cleared in the cool breeze of the beach and a swim in the heavenly water. She would not backslide. She had vowed to approach her life with less fear. Taking risks sometimes meant making the wrong call. Getting hurt. And Aristos had always been a wild card.

Aristos's last guest left on a Cessna just after three. Only David remained beside him, waiting for his helicopter to take him to Athens, then Las Vegas.

"So how was Dimitri?"

"Hedging. He still wouldn't give me a straight answer at breakfast. Says he needs to look at his portfolio."

"The offer's still open. I can work my channels…"

Aristos shook his head. "He'll come around."

David raked a hand through his thick graying hair. "You'll pull this one out of the fire, Aristos. I've no doubt about it."

A faint smile touched his mouth. "It will be my biggest

magic act to date. Maintaining funding for an illusionary casino that may never be built."

"It will." David sank his hands into his pockets. "I like her, Aristos."

"Who?"

"You know who I'm talking about." His mentor shook his head. "I worry sometimes you think you don't deserve happiness. That you consider it unattainable to you."

"Maybe it is."

"And maybe you're just afraid to reach for it."

Maybe it wasn't worth it. He'd watched his family fall apart under the weight of the burdens it carried—financially, emotionally—his mother turning into a shadow of her former self when life had worn away at the very edges of her. Had watched the rosy glow slip from his life as a so-called revolutionary when it became clear the term was only used to perpetuate the violence, the control, those in charge had sought to exercise over them all as foot soldiers.

Happiness, those myths the storytellers liked to weave, they had always turned out to be lies for him. *How could you want what you didn't even believe existed?*

Returning to his office after David left, their conversation continued to dominate his head. *Content* was a state of being he could get on board with. Money went a long way toward providing that. Except he didn't seem to even have that state of mind in his possession anymore. Being around Alex reflected back at him the image of a man he wasn't sure he wanted to be any longer, a problem when you thought maybe that was all you had in you.

He'd thrown most, but not all, of his dark past at her and she hadn't blinked. Didn't seem to think any less of him for it. He wondered what she'd think if she knew the truth. How he'd walked away from the people who'd needed him most, not once, but twice. How being the man who always put himself first made him a selfish creature who wasn't about to change his spots.

He put his feet up on his desk and closed his eyes as he waited for Carin to put his call through. Allowed himself to consider the implications of last night after spending all day avoiding them. Alex had claimed her virginity changed nothing between them, that it had been her decision to make and she'd wanted her first time to be with him.

He could convince himself she had been right, it was that simple, that the damage was done and the only way was forward. The question was what *was* the way forward? Either he shut this down, likely the path he should take, or he made the conscious choice to do exactly what Alex had proposed—see where this thing between them went in a time-limited, short-term affair.

Expelling a breath, he hit the intercom and asked for an espresso to go with his call. His brain didn't seem to be in working order, because the only thing that did seem to be computing about this whole mess he'd predicted so accurately was that, in his lust, he'd recklessly claimed something that hadn't been his to own—the innocence of a royal. There would be consequences; he just didn't know what they were yet.

Alex was debating whether to go down to dinner alone or have it in her room when Aristos showed up at her door. Propped up against the jamb, all earthly male in khaki shorts and another of those T-shirts that showed off his muscles, it was all she could do to look completely unaffected.

"Everyone gone?"

He nodded. "Up for dinner?"

She eyed him. "Are you still angry with me?"

His mouth curved. "My feelings toward you are a whole lot of things, but anger isn't one of them."

"You walked out last night…"

"Because I needed to think."

Right. Where was that anger that had fueled her all day? The aloofness she so desperately needed? She looked down at the sundress she wore. "I'm not dressed for dinner."

His gaze slid over her. "You could wear a garbage bag and still look utterly edible, Princess. Grab your shoes. Sneakers, actually. We're going sailing."

"Sailing?"

"Thought you might like to see the sunset from the water. Chef made us dinner."

Her disobedient pulse fluttered. A sunset cruise would be intimate… But perhaps exactly what they needed at the moment to resolve last night. Slipping on sneakers and sunglasses, she walked with him to the beach. His gaze rested on her as they walked along the sand toward the dinghy waiting for them. "You look pale."

"Headache. It's going now."

"The champagne?"

"I didn't drink enough for that." Fire filled her cheeks. He'd consumed *her* before that had gone very far.

For once he made no smart comeback. Guided her instead to the motorized dinghy that took them out to the forty-five-foot sailboat waiting for them.

Once they were on the water, she found herself immersed in the rush of the wind. While anything but an accomplished sailor, she knew which sail was which and made a decent team member for Aristos, who *was* an extremely competent sailor, athletic and commanding as he guided them in a loop of the surrounding islands.

When they finally dropped anchor in a perfect little cove, the sun beginning to sink into the horizon in yet another of those spectacular blood-orange sunsets, another set of muscles she hadn't used in a while was making itself known. Wincing, she sank to the deck.

"Sore?" Aristos asked.

"Yes. And thirsty."

He unearthed a cooler from below deck, handed her a bottle and took a beer for himself. She eyed the vodka-based cranberry drink with amusement. "A girl drink for me?"

He moved his gaze over her in one of those totally inappropriate looks that made her breath catch in her throat. "Yes," he drawled, "definitely a girl."

Pinpricks of heat unfurled beneath her skin. She took a sip of the surprisingly tasty drink to cover her fluster. When Aristos stripped off his T-shirt to enjoy the dying rays of the sun, she followed suit. As far as bikinis went, hers was modest, far from attention-seeking. Aristos, on the other hand, sprawled out beside her, beer in hand, was the definition of the term in dark blue swim trunks, his long, bronzed limbs all tight, corded muscle. A couple of days' worth of stubble lining his cheeks and jaw added to his dangerous appeal.

"We should talk about last night."

She pulled in a breath. "Yes."

"First of all," he said, training that deadly dark gaze on her, "I wanted to say that you were amazing last night. Last night was amazing."

Her stomach clenched. "I thought what happened might have ruined it for you."

"It caught me off guard. I did not expect it."

"I was going to tell you but it didn't seem like the right time once we—"

"—consumed each other," he offered drily.

"Yes."

"Are you worried you disappointed me?"

She nodded.

"No chance of that, angel. It was off the charts."

A warmth engulfed her, radiating through her chest. "So why walk out?"

A long moment passed. "I'm insanely attracted to you," he said finally. "I care about you, Alex. I think that's clear. But anything beyond that, I can't offer. My longest relationship was three months—shorter than many of my contract negotiations."

Her jaw tightened. "To use your words, we've been through this. I've already told you I'm not looking for a relationship. I have a whole new life ahead of me I need to focus on. And second, as I said last night, me being a virgin doesn't change anything about our agreement. I was waiting for the right time. The right experience."

"Yes, but it creates…expectations."

"What expectations?"

"You gave me something special, Alex."

"Frightening, you mean."

"That's not what I said."

"It's what you meant. If you'd left my room any faster, you would have been running."

He sighed. "I'm not frightened. I'm concerned I'm going to hurt you. Relationships are messy, complicated entanglements I prefer to avoid."

"And now that we've reinforced the fact that I'm *not* looking for a relationship, where does that leave us?"

His dark gaze glittered. "I think that's up to you, Princess. As long as you're clear on who and what I am."

The antagonism that had been simmering just below the surface roared back to life. "I think that would be a difficult thing for me to swear allegiance to when you hide yourself behind your walls, Aristos. When you run at the first sign of intimacy. I wonder if *you* know who you are."

The glitter in his eyes intensified. "Oh, I know who I am, angel. An unashamedly, unapologetically solitary man.

Overtly ambitious and perhaps a bit spiritually corrupt. There is no redemption for me."

She blinked. Took a sip of her drink. "Actually," she said, "I think you forgot an inspirational success story for those who've walked your path, a person who gives back to others in need, a man who has a big heart he refuses to acknowledge."

A cynical twist curved his mouth. "I should make you my PR person. You'd have me on the most admired CEO list in no time, something even my own PR team can't seem to do."

She shook her head as he deflected again. "Nice try, Aristos. But I have your number now."

"Do you?" He downed a long swallow of beer, swiped his palm across his mouth, set the bottle aside and leaned back on his elbows. "Give it to me. I'm fascinated to hear what you think."

She took a deep breath. "I think David Tennyson might have picked you up off that street in Athens and helped build you a new life, an immensely successful life, but somewhere along the way, likely far before that, you closed yourself off from the broken relationships and promises that defined your life. You told yourself that love and relationships weren't to be trusted, were messy, complicated entanglements. To you they only meant hurt.

"You deflect people with sarcasm," she continued, "when they try to get close. You carry on your 'transactional' relationships because they are of no threat to you. You are a lone wolf, and you like to keep it that way."

She held his gaze. Found it full of an emotion she couldn't read. "How am I doing?"

Deadly accurate. Aristos waved a hand at her. "Keep going. I'll give my analysis at the end."

"Last night you ran because of the connection we share

as much as from taking my virginity. Because you've let me in and you don't like it. Because it breaks all your rules."

She sat back on her elbows and took a sip of her drink, apparently finished with her excellent summation of him. Her rosy cheeks, the nervous half glance she threw him, suggested she worried she might have gone too far. He thought that if it had been any other person on the planet, it might have been. But not her.

"Very perceptive," he drawled. "I like the lone-wolf analogy. But don't be fooled by our connection, Princess. It will only take you so far."

"I don't doubt it. But since we are only having an affair, if you've decided that's still going to happen between us, it's irrelevant, isn't it?"

He eyed her. Took another swig of his beer. "I feel like I've created a monster."

She gave him a self-satisfied smile. "Take the plunge, Aristos. Make the call."

Every muscle in his body coiled at the challenge. He was not unaware that indulging in what was in front of him meant taking his fledgling ability to be intimate with another person to the next level, but he couldn't have stopped himself if he'd tried.

"Get over here," he murmured.

Her lashes lowered. "I don't take orders from you."

"Yes, you do. Now get over here."

A flare of excitement lit those beautiful blue eyes. Setting her drink down, she pressed her palms to the deck and shimmied toward him. He snagged an arm around her waist and lifted her atop him so her legs were wrapped around him. His gaze rested on her quivering full lower lip, lust tightening his insides.

"I'm feeling a bit spiritually bankrupt," he drawled, lifting his gaze to hers. "You'd better send in the reinforcements."

Her mouth curved. "I thought you were a lone wolf."

"Don't you ever hear them howl at night?"

Her breathtakingly beautiful smile blinded him as he bent his head and took her mouth in a hot, searing kiss. Her hands clasped his jaw, anchored herself as he devoured her with a hunger he'd kept in check last night. She was with him all the way, arching into his hands when he stripped off her bikini top, moaning when he rolled her nipples between his fingers.

Then it wasn't enough, not nearly enough, because he needed to own her as much as she owned him in that moment as he pushed himself into uncharted territory.

Sliding his palm down her flat, quivering stomach, he moved his fingers beneath the waistband of her bikini bottoms and cupped the warmth at the heart of her.

Her breathing fractured, those long, silky dark lashes lifting to reveal a brilliant blue. "Aristos," she whispered, "we can't— We're—"

"—in the middle of the Aegean."

"Yes, but—"

He squeezed her soft flesh. Stroked her silky skin. A stifled gasp filled his ear.

"Like that, angel?"

"Y-yes."

His thumb found her core, rocking against her in a gentle rhythm that had her moving against his hand. Eyes closed, mouth parted, cheeks flushed, she was the hottest thing he'd ever seen, turning him hard as a stone.

She must have known he was watching her. Her lashes fluttered open, gaze meeting the heat in his. He increased the pressure of his thumb, moving in tight, deliberate circles now, his eyes seducing her as surely as his fingers.

A frown of concentration crossed her brow, her nails digging into his biceps as her orgasm built. Slipping his fingers inside her, he stroked her to the edge. *Ei sai poly omora,"* he whispered, cupping her nape and bringing his mouth down on hers as he increased the rhythm of his fingers. *You're beautiful.*

A fractured moan left her lips, her hips pushing against his hand. Sinking his fingers deeper inside her, he whispered, "Come for me, angel."

Closing her eyes, she melted into him. Rocked harder until she came apart on a low cry he swallowed with a conqueror's satisfaction.

Fumbling in his pocket, he found a condom. He set her away from him long enough to roll it on, then lifted her with one arm and brought her down on him, his fingers pushing aside the thin strip of her bikini bottoms and guiding his shaft to her slick, hot flesh.

Her eyes widened, nails biting into his flesh as he penetrated her snug channel.

"Aristos. You're so big... I—"

"Slow," he muttered thickly. "We take it slow, *glykeia mou.*"

She closed her eyes. Trusted him with her body. Gradually, her body accepted his, melted around him until he was buried deep inside her. She opened her eyes then, an expression of wonder in those blue orbs that rocked him to his core.

Slowly, gently, he gripped her hips, moving her up and down on him, claiming her with every gasp-inducing thrust of his body. His eyes on hers, he reached between them and rubbed his thumb over the pleasure point at the center of her. Stroked her into another release.

When she came in a shudder, he claimed his own pleasure. A few quick thrusts was all it took, her pulsing, tight flesh shaking his body in a violent release that stole his breath.

She is mine. This time there was no going back.

CHAPTER TWELVE

ARISTOS TRACED THE perfect sloping line of Alex's voluptuous hip with a light touch designed to deify rather than wake. He'd had her in his bed for three days and still he couldn't get enough of her. It was like going to the well to drink and discovering you had a never-ending thirst that was impossible to slake. Like discovering something that might finally make you feel whole if you consumed enough of it.

In spite of that thought, or perhaps because of it, he eased himself away from her and slid his legs over the side of the bed. He was going to pin Dimitri Smirnov down to a meeting today. Spinning his wheels, wondering if the Russian was going to pull out on him, was killing his head, destroying his productivity. It needed to be settled. Cast in stone.

Showering and dressing, he left temptation alone, grabbed a croissant from the kitchen and made his way to his office. Carin greeted him, handed him a stack of messages and got up to get his espresso. Wandering into his office, he made for his PC.

Carin backtracked and came to the door. "Were you just whistling?"

"Whistling?" He frowned. "I don't whistle."

"That's what I thought." She gave him a look. "You *were* whistling."

"First time for everything. Anything urgent in this?" He waved the stack of messages at her.

"June. She said she sent you an urgent email."

Since his PR person bothered him only when something was truly important, he went right to his email, immediately thinking there'd been a crisis at one of his hotels. The last one had been a couple of rare birds who'd taken up residence in the facing of his London property. Threatened with eviction, the entire bird-loving population of London had revolted, placard-carrying activists and all. The birds had stayed.

He clicked open June's email, bracing himself for a political nightmare. It was a nightmare, all right, but not a political one. The photo June had sent made his head buzz. It was of him and Alex from that night on the boat, an intimate photo of them, Alex half naked, her legs wrapped around him.

His heart sank further as he read the caption from the European entertainment website it had been posted to.

Princess Aleksandra busy canoodling with billionaire Aristos Nicolades in the Aegean while Akathinia sits in wait.

Canoodling? Who used that word?

Thee mou. The enormity of the disaster sank through him as he sat back in his chair and wiped a palm across his brow. How had this happened? Paparazzi couldn't access the island. It was impossible. It had to have been a staff member.

His vision went red. "Carin."

She came in with his espresso. Took in his expression. "I take it the whistling is over?"

"Get Yolande in here *now*. And Rolf." His head of security.

His PA departed. He took a deep, fortifying sip of the coffee to kick-start his brain. The damage was done, but he could inflict pain on whoever had done this. And he *would* find them.

He was picking up the phone to call June in New York when his cell phone buzzed. Glancing at the screen, he replaced the receiver. *Nikandros.* He contemplated the buzzing phone, a tight feeling in his chest. He could ignore it, gather a game plan, then talk to the king. Or he could pick it up and get it over with.

He picked it up. "Nik."

"You have sixty seconds to explain why I shouldn't fly there right now and kill you."

"I care about her, Nik."

"*Try again, Nicolades.* You've never cared about a woman in your life."

"I care about her."

Silence.

He rubbed a hand to his temple. "You were the one who insisted she come here. *I* didn't want her here."

"And it was too much of a stretch to keep your hands off her? Off *one woman*, Aristos."

"Why?" Aristos wanted to hear Nik say it. That he wasn't good enough for Aleksandra. That he was below her.

"You know why. You are the most notorious womanizer on the face of the planet."

He digested that. Wondered for the first time if that was the core of Nik's issue with him, rather than his bloodline.

He closed his eyes. "It's done, Nik. But I intend to make it right."

"How?"

"We'll marry, of course."

Another long silence. *Had he just said that?* The *M*-word?

"I haven't given you my permission."

Ah, there it was. He raked a hand through his hair. "You know it's the right answer."

Another silence. "Get your PR team in contact with

mine. Put a lid on this. Meanwhile, Alex stays on Larikos. The press can't get to her there, and I need to focus on Idas. The rumor is he's had a stroke."

His heart lifted for the first time since he'd seen that damning photo. "Substantiated?"

"We're working on it."

He prayed it was true. Crown Prince Kostas of Carnelia was a known proponent of peace and democracy. It would be a godsend for the country and for his $2.5 billion investment. "Nik—"

"I need to think." The line went dead.

He pulled the phone away from his ear, a knot growing in his stomach at what he'd just done. Getting bigger by the minute. He should have ignored the call. Should have gotten his thoughts together, made a plan. Instead he'd just announced he was marrying Alex. He, who had once called marriage hell on earth, had just committed himself to that very institution.

Rising from his chair, he paced to the window, espresso in hand. Looked out at the glorious, picture-perfect vista he so often took for granted. Was too busy to even enjoy. He'd spent three of those sun-soaked, unparalleled Larikos days with Alex, working, yes, because he needed to keep things moving, but also using the opportunity to take a step back. To allow himself a breather from the obsession with business that had consumed his life.

He'd found himself more even-keeled, without his usual restless vibe, a perspective settling over him, a contentment. Perhaps those obsessions that had fueled him all these years had blinded him to other things…to the things he'd told himself he couldn't have.

He rubbed a palm over his jaw. Could he have them with Alex? Was this the solution to a problem he'd already known he'd had?

He watched the sun reflect off an impossibly blue sea.

Surprisingly, the idea of marrying Alex didn't fill him with horror. His interest in meaningless assignations had waned months before. Having a beautiful, intelligent wife by his side to fill the empty life he'd been leading held appeal, a woman for whom his desire was showing no signs of abating, who seemed to be chipping away at his cynicism with every moment he spent with her, making him feel almost human again.

And yet, he wondered, how far could he take it? Was he deluding himself he could ever be *that* man? The one who deposited his briefcase on the kitchen floor, received a kiss from his wife, went back to work the next day and did it over and over again? The man who stuck? Nik certainly seemed to be questioning it. He hadn't even given him his permission to marry Alex.

Memories, too close to the surface in recent days, bubbled their way to the surface. His last epic battle with his father before he'd left home for good…

This family is better off without you, Aristos. You have no substance, no honor. Go waste your life away with those infidels. You are one of them now.

And he had been. He would have been anything to get away from the toxic atmosphere at home. Even if it meant leaving everything he knew behind, including the brothers and sisters he'd loved. Even if it meant cutting those ties for their own safety, keeping them away from the lawless men he associated with.

But there had been more. He'd been angry, so angry at his mother for choosing his no-good father over him, for allowing him to turn him out. Bitter to the core. That was when the murkiness of the street had climbed inside and claimed his soul.

A text from June buzzed his mobile. Pulled him out of the past, the bitter taste of regret staining his mouth. He swung away from the window to answer it. Whether he deserved Alex, whether he was husband of the year material, was irrelevant. What mattered was repairing this situation before it spiraled out of control.

He'd been gone only hours and already she missed him.

Lifting her gaze from the text blurring in front of her, Alex acknowledged that disconcerting thought. She'd started a business plan for Nina as they'd begun to define their partnership, the need to plan her future a necessary distraction from her present, a grounding force she desperately needed given her current reality that involved long, hot, heady nights with Aristos and the very real fact that she was half in love with him. Possibly more.

Her risk-taking had taken her down a road she knew it wasn't wise to go, but it really wasn't the sort of road you just turned back from. Not when you thought the man in question might finally be letting his barriers down, slowly but surely. When you saw a potential there that was too bright and seductive to ignore.

With every day that passed, her decision to leave Stygos seemed more right. She still got homesick, still missed so much about its peaceful allure, but she realized now how much living she had to do. How her aversion to risk-taking had limited her experiences. And Aristos was a big part of that.

It was disconcerting how much she wanted to be the one to do the same for him. To be the one to open *his* world up—to show him what he was missing by cutting himself off from his emotions. To make him believe some people could be trusted, that *she* could be trusted.

Dangerous thinking indeed, but not enough to prevent her from putting on her shoes and making her way over to his office with the excuse that she needed a break. Peeking inside, she found him on the phone. He beckoned to her with a crooked finger. She walked in, perched herself on the windowsill and waited for him to finish barking out instructions on how to enter the airspace at Larikos.

"Who's coming?" she asked when he hung up.

"A jeweler."

"A jeweler?" She frowned. "Why?"

Aristos sat back in his chair and patted the corner of his desk. She eyed the open door. His mouth curled. "As appealing as that idea is," he drawled, "we have a situation we need to deal with."

It was then that she noticed the edge to him. The ruffled hair, the tight set of his mouth, the rapid-fire intensity to him.

She slid onto the edge of the desk, a feeling of unease whispering across her skin. "What is it?"

"The night we were on the yacht, someone took a photo of us."

She froze, graphic images of what they'd done that night filling her head. "You said no one could get anywhere near the island."

"They can't. A staff member must have taken it."

A staff member? Her stomach sank, a sick feeling engulfing her. "What kind of a photo?"

"The incriminating kind." He sat forward and clicked a button. Her brain went into lockdown. The photo on his computer screen had been taken with a long-range lens, her in Aristos's arms, legs wrapped around him, stark naked except for her bikini bottoms, head tossed back as she looked up at him. *Thee mou.* Her mouth went dry. The angle of the photo had been artfully done so nothing indecent was showing, but it was the look on her face that sent heat rushing to her cheeks. She looked...love struck.

"Where?" she whispered. "Where did you get this?"

"A European gossip site. But according to my PR person the rights have been sold to a handful of other daily newspapers."

"Can you stop it?"

"We're trying, but injunctions take time."

"What are we going to do?" Her voice had risen now. "I am *naked* in that photo, Aristos. I am a *princess*. You need to do something."

"I *am* doing something." His dangerously low tone warned her to pull it back a notch. "I've done about fifteen things in the last two hours."

She pressed her knuckles to her cheek. "I'm sorry. This is a shock."

"Nikandros," he said evenly, "called first thing this morning."

The blood drained from her face. "What did he say?"

"That I had sixty seconds to give him a reason not to kill me."

Theos. She stared at him. "And how did you…explain it?"

He calmly took a sip of his coffee. "The funny thing about a photo like that. It explains itself… So I didn't so much explain it as offer a solution."

She didn't like the hard glint in his eyes. "Which was?"

"We marry."

Her mouth dropped open. "You— I— *No.* That's not a solution."

"By all means," he said, his voice dripping with sarcasm, "come up with an alternative. I'm all ears."

She swallowed hard. "We simply explain to Nik things got a little…out of hand and I'm sure he will understand."

"And do we tell that to the rest of the world, too? A short little concise press release? *After lusting after each other for weeks, Aristos and Alex took matters into their own hands and—*"

"Aristos."

"You need a better plan than that, angel. Akathinia is still under the threat of war. It does not look good."

She shook her head. "Nik will calm down. It will be fine."

"Did I mention he threatened to kill me?"

She bit her lip. "He didn't mean that. He was angry."

"Yes, Princess, very angry, which is why we are going to defuse the situation. Now. This afternoon, in fact."

"I am not marrying you. This is insanity."

"Insane but unavoidable."

She stared at his determined expression. *Diavole*, but he was serious! The phone call she had walked in on flashed through her head. "Why is the jeweler coming?"

"So you can pick the largest, most outrageously beautiful engagement ring you want."

"Oh, no," she said, rising. "We are not getting engaged."

He snared an arm around her waist and pulled her down onto his lap. "Nothing is going to defuse this situation but an engagement. Nothing is going to defuse *Nik* but an engagement. So wrap your head around it."

She stared at him, attempting to process the unreality unfolding around her. And suddenly, she understood what he wasn't saying. He did business with Nik. Nik had granted him his casino license. Nik could also take it away.

"Let me talk to him," she said. "I'm sure he will see reason."

"Alex," he said softly. "It's not just Nik. It's your reputation you have to consider now. You are not a normal citizen anymore. You are a princess. The rules aren't the same. You know it and I know it. We're both to blame for this. We need to own the consequences."

There it was—those consequences he'd been talking about. *And, oh, how right he'd been.*

"You don't want to get married. You swore you'd never do it." She poked a finger against his chest. "You'll be miserable. Why would I want to commit myself to that?"

"I've had a couple more hours to wrap my head around

this than you have," he said grimly. "I'm about ten steps ahead. Besides," he said, shifting her so her bottom fit more securely within the span of his hips, "there could be worse things than having you in my bed...*every* night."

Her chest tightened. "This is not funny."

"Believe me, I'm feeling a lot of things right now, Princess, but humor isn't one of them."

She took a deep breath. "Aristos—this is crazy. We can't do this. You don't want this."

"It doesn't matter what I want." He tucked a stray curl behind her ear. "We are good together. We knew we had a problem—now we have a solution."

She shook her head. "You're mad. It's not enough for marriage."

"Why not? I find myself...bored with my current lifestyle. It can't go on forever. We could do good things together."

Her back stiffened. "So you want me to marry you to *amuse* you?"

"Yes," he said silkily, "that and many more things."

"No." She scrambled off his lap. "There has to be another way. I need to think."

Unfortunately, thinking didn't provide solutions. Particularly after Nik's phone call that afternoon in which he was short and to the point. The family didn't need any more scandals; an engagement would be ideal. They would take an engagement photo after she'd chosen her ring today and send it out along with a press release tomorrow morning announcing her and Aristos's engagement. The strategy was to replace the scandalous coverage with the happy news of a pending royal match.

Alex didn't even think about refusing. She was too busy staring at the wall wondering how she'd gotten herself into this situation. Cringing at the disappointment that had stained her brother's tone. Another Dimitriou royal scandal—a PR nightmare for the palace.

Her stomach twisted, tying itself into a tight knot. How could she possibly have been so careless? So unthinking of her position when her mother's lesson should have served as the biggest one of them all?

Three hours later, she found herself trying on rings from one of London's most exclusive jewelers. Numbly she chose a square-cut sapphire surrounded by diamonds, requested by her soon-to-be fiancé because it reminded him of her spectacular eyes.

Aristos put it on her finger, the cold slide of metal against her overheated skin sending a shiver down her spine. It fit perfectly because, of course, Aristos always got the details right. Which meant it stayed there. Which meant they were engaged.

If it wasn't the romantic proposal she'd always dreamed of, with her suitor down on one knee, she was too dazed to much acknowledge it.

When the photographer left, she and Aristos sat down to a late dinner and a bottle of champagne that tasted flat to her frozen senses. She told herself this wasn't set in stone, that once the furor died down, an engagement could always be broken. Couldn't it? But she knew in her heart that part of her decision had stemmed from her feelings for Aristos. Because she was in love with him, and maybe they *could* make this work.

"What?" Aristos arched a brow at her when she was unusually silent during the meal.

"Nothing. Did you get Dimitri tied down?"

"Yes. He and Galina are going to come stay this weekend with us."

"*This* weekend?"

"Yes."

It was the last thing she needed, to host the Russians

when she was grappling with all of this, but she forced a smile to her lips. "That's a good sign, then."

"Who knows with him."

She told herself not to interfere, but the research she'd done on the Smirnovs had been too revealing: rumors of drug-taking in his clubs abounded, that he perhaps participated in that drug trade highly debated.

She shot him a look. "He's a bad man, Aristos. Why do you do business with him?"

"Our dealings are purely financial."

"Yes, but him being an investor reflects on you. On your business."

His jaw hardened. "Do you know how many squeaky-clean sources of money there are in the world? Very few."

"So you choose to look the other way?"

His lip curled. "Are you picking a fight, Princess? And here I thought we were celebrating."

Being railroaded into an engagement was putting her in a funny mood. She pointed her glass at him. "Why is this casino so important to you? Why, with all the other properties you have, is Akathinia such an obsession?"

His gaze narrowed. "Because it is the jewel of the Mediterranean...because the world's elite vacation there...because no one's been able to crack it before now. When it's done it will put any other hotel and casino on the planet to shame."

"And," she pointed out, "it's your roots. It will prove to those who gave up on you how far you've come. That they were wrong about you."

He smiled, but it didn't reach his eyes. "Putting words in my mouth, Alex? Maybe it's not so insightful as that. Every developer in the world would kill to build on Akathinia."

She conceded the point with a dip of her head. Pushed the piece of fish she hadn't the appetite for around her plate, her engagement ring sparkling in the muted lighting.

"You done with that?" His low drawl brought her head

up. "Because if you are, I thought we could continue the celebration in private."

The look of intent in his sinful eyes vibrated through her. She lifted her chin. "I have a headache."

His gaze sharpened. "Is that so?"

She lifted a shoulder. "A tension one from today."

He threw his napkin on the table. "Good thing, then, that I am an expert at working the knots out."

She eyed him. He held out a hand and pulled her to her feet. They stood toe to toe, taking each other's measure. "It's been a long day," he murmured. "You get a massage. Anything more than that, you can let me know. You won't ever get anything you don't want from me, Alex."

Her heart went into free fall. Feelings she couldn't suppress bubbled to the surface, enveloping her in a warmth, a hot headiness, that threw her mixed feelings into a tempest. "That would be perfect," she said softly. "My shoulders are a mess."

Aristos's suite was bathed in a muted glow when they arrived, dozens of candles burning from tapered silver holders scattered around the room's sleek, luxurious surfaces. Roses of dark pink and red tumbled from vases, filling the air with an intoxicating aroma.

Her gaze moved to Aristos's. "You did this?"

"I asked Yolande to." He nodded to the bathroom, where a rose-scented bath had been drawn. "Go take a bath first. It'll help with the knots."

She stripped off her dress and underwear and stepped into the heavenly water. It did wonders for her stiff muscles and disposition. When she climbed out and wrapped herself in the silk robe hanging on the door, Aristos was typing out a message on his phone. He nodded toward the bed. "Be right there."

She perched on the edge. He tapped out the rest of the

message and tossed the phone onto the dresser, his gaze eating her up as he closed the distance between them.

"You know what I was thinking that first night we were here," he said huskily, his fingers toying with the lapels on her robe, "when you had that blue wrap dress on…"

She shook her head, eyes glued to his.

"That I wanted to unwrap you like a present. That you are so beautiful, any man lucky enough to get his hands on you should savor the opportunity. Recognize his good luck."

A shiver went through her. He captured her left hand, blazing with his sapphire on it, and brought her fingers to his mouth. "That makes me an exceedingly lucky man tonight, angel."

The maelstrom of emotions swirling through her intensified, until she felt as if she were in the eye of the storm. "Always?" she asked quietly. "Are you always going to feel that way? Or will it fade as 'evolutionary history dictates'?"

His mouth twisted. "I'd say we're both in uncharted territory here. The truth is, we fit. I know when to give you the push you need and you—" her heart sat suspended as he searched for words "—you show me what's possible. You show me the things I want to have."

Her insides dissolved. She saw it then in his dark-as-night eyes, the infinite possibilities for them. The spectacular and never-ending kind, if she was patient enough to wait for them. Brave enough.

He reached for the sash of her robe. Tugged it open. Her breath caught in her throat as he took her in, his gaze tracing a line down to her breasts, to the vee at the apex of her thighs, down over the curve of her legs to her coral-tipped toes. It turned her insides to liquid.

"I think," she said breathlessly, "the bath worked out those knots."

His mouth curved. "The head?"

"Better."

She waited, nipples hardening, body anticipating his caresses. Still he didn't touch her.

"What do you want?" he asked quietly, eyes on hers.

She stepped closer. "You."

It was like sealing her fate, the kiss that followed. Gentle, passionate, never ending—it was all of those things. His hands moved to her shoulders, slipped the robe from her. Her fingers dispensed with the button on his shorts. When she reached inside his boxers and closed her fingers over the hard, thick length of him, he was velvet over steel.

Tentative, then gaining confidence, she explored him. Stroked him. He closed his fingers over hers, tightened her grip, showed her how he liked it. It was so erotic, heated her blood to a slow simmer to do this with him. To share this with him.

His hand at the small of her back, he pushed her toward the dresser, setting her hands on its polished surface. Her gaze met his in the mirror. "Stay there," he murmured.

The ripping sound of a condom wrapper pierced her sensual haze. It stoked her blood even hotter. He came back to her, ran his palms down her spine to cup her buttocks. His foot nudged her feet apart. She allowed herself to be put where he wanted her, the blood roaring in her ears as she watched him behind her. He sank his teeth into her shoulder in a wicked caress.

His palm cupped her between her thighs. She was ready for him, more than ready. His low rasp of approval as he parted her silky flesh sent another shiver through her.

"*Thee mou*, but you do something to me." He sank his fingers inside her. She moved into his touch, reaching for him. He pushed her hands back onto the dresser. "Leave them there."

She did. If his intent was to make her vulnerable, to

leave her wide-open to him, to demonstrate how completely he owned her, he had succeeded. Her breath left her in a gasp as he placed one hand on her buttock and brought himself to rest against her moist, willing flesh.

"Arch your back," he commanded, eyes burning into hers. She did. He slid into her with a slow penetration that set every nerve ending in her body screaming for more.

"Aristos."

"Look at me, angel. I've got you."

She anchored herself in his gaze. His hands cupped her buttocks as he stroked his way inside her. Harder, deeper, until she could feel him everywhere, touching the very heart of her. He was so big and powerful, the places he hit inside her so intensely pleasurable, she started to shake under his hands.

He leaned forward, capturing her earlobe in his teeth. Scoring it lightly. "Relax, angel."

Relax? She was ready to beg for him to touch her, to push her over the edge, but it was his body that did it instead. The power of him that made her tighten with a desperate clench, the throb of her orgasm radiating out from her center as a scream left her throat.

He gripped her hips tighter and thrust inside her, pleasure exploding in his eyes. Just when she thought it couldn't get any better—it always did.

He carried her to the bed when they'd recovered their breath. The weight of her engagement ring felt foreign as she curled up against him, her hand tucked against her cheek. Made her feel fidgety, restless.

Aristos pulled her tighter against him. "You're mine now," he said roughly. "Forget about the rest."

How could she? The shock in her mother's voice when she'd called to give her the news replayed itself in her head. Her pointed question as to whether she knew what she was doing with Aristos.

She was taking the longest of long shots. Risking it all for a man who didn't commit. Who'd sworn he wouldn't. And yet with the slide of Aristos's hand against her back, sleep consumed her.

CHAPTER THIRTEEN

"THE SASSICAIA OR the Excelsus?" Aristos's French chef lifted a brow. "Or both...?"

Alex surveyed the two bottles of wine. You really couldn't go wrong with either with the meal they were serving Dimitri and Galina Smirnov, but she was being a perfectionist because it was so important to Aristos, and he had put her in charge.

"I think both," she said, "but let me check with Aristos."

She made her way to the casino, the afternoon shower having given way to sunshine in anticipation of their guests' arrival. She had been happy to help with the dinner given the insanity of the past few days...the field day the press was having with both the nude and official engagement photos, although that sport seemed to play second fiddle to the fun they were having predicting how long the playboy billionaire's marriage would last.

They had been making bets. Taking polls. It was enough to make her think she *had* lost her wits in agreeing to marry him.

Carin's chair was empty, her fiancé on the phone when she walked into Aristos's office, his New York lawyer's voice coming through the speakerphone.

She sat on the corner of Carin's desk and waited, not wanting to hurry him as he and the lawyer went through a contract. Aristos, efficient as always, plowed through the terms in minutes. When they were done, his lawyer asked him if he needed anything else.

"Start working on a prenup for me."

Her shoulders stiffened.

"Sure. You got a ballpark figure in mind?"

Aristos named an outrageous number that made her mouth drop open.

"That's very...generous."

"I don't intend to give it away. I'm a lucky man. Not to mention Alex will bring considerable assets to the table herself. It's an advantageous union from all angles. A politically advantageous union for Nicolades Inc."

"No doubt," agreed the lawyer.

Her stomach tightened. *A politically advantageous union?* She told herself to focus on the "lucky man" part. But did that have more to do with what she brought to the table personally or her lineage as a Constantinides?

Aristos ended the call. She stayed where she was for a good couple of minutes so it wouldn't be clear she'd overheard the conversation, then slid off the desk and made her way into his office. She didn't mention what she'd heard. Wasn't sure why not. Maybe because she thought she was being oversensitive, that just because Aristos needed Nik's casino license for his current obsession it didn't mean that's all *they* were.

But it festered as she dressed for dinner that evening in a silver-beaded cocktail dress. Aristos came up behind her in the mirror as she stood choosing her jewelry.

"I haven't seen this one yet." He rested his hands on her hips. "I like it."

The smoky, intimate tone he'd undoubtedly used on every one of the women the papers had mentioned as notable exes inspired the usual flock of butterflies in her stomach, but she held herself stiff beneath his hands. "Stella chose it."

He gave her a long look in the mirror. "Anything wrong? More outrageous press coverage?"

Too much to count. She shook her head. "You should get ready. We need to go."

He surveyed the carefully schooled expression on her face. Pulled her back into him and set his lips to her jaw. "You playing hard to get, angel? I could like that game."

She pushed against him and stepped out of his arms. "No. I still need to do my hair."

The look he scorched her with could have stripped paint from a car, but he stepped back, made his way to the wardrobe and acquired a shirt. A fine pair they were going to make, she thought, grimacing, as she gathered her hair on top of her head. Aristos the powder keg in advance of the Russian's visit, her distinctly *off*.

The Smirnovs were waiting for them on the main terrace. Dimitri, a tall, thin, elegant figure with a sharp face and eyes that missed nothing, pressed a kiss to both her cheeks.

"Congratulations on your engagement. And here I had no idea you were a princess."

"We weren't broadcasting the fact given the political situation."

"Understandable."

Alex greeted Galina more warmly while her fiancé shook his nemesis's hand. They sat down to drinks, then dinner. Galina asked about her and Aristos's wedding plans. She tried to focus on the innocuous conversation, but her attention was captured by the cat-and-mouse game going on between the two men.

Aristos was direct and to the point. Dimitri was non-committal and evasive, a game player. One who flouted the law and who could someday become a liability to her fiancé, but he wouldn't acknowledge it. Not that she was anything but polite to the Russian, if coolly so, but as the dinner wore on, her patience wore thin.

"I'm opening a new club in Moscow in October." Dimitri

directed the comment at Alex as dessert was served. "You should come."

"I'm afraid I'm not much into clubbing," she returned evenly.

Dimitri lifted a dark brow. "Oh, but this one is like no other. Lions in cages. Waitstaff suspended from the ceiling. It's something to see."

"I'm quite sure you're right."

Dimitri gave her a long look. Aristos gave her knee a squeeze.

She could have stood up and given a cheer when the meal was over. But it wasn't to end there, unfortunately. Dimitri declared himself in favor of a nightcap. The staff relieved for the night, Aristos went off to procure a bottle of brandy. When Galina got up to use the ladies' room, Alex rose to follow her. Dimitri put a hand on her arm. "Stay and keep me company."

What could she do? She suggested they move to the comfortable lounge area that overlooked the sea. That used up some time. When she sat down on the sofa, Dimitri sat beside her.

"I get the feeling you don't like me, Princess."

She widened her eyes. "Why would you think that?"

"I've asked you to call me Dimitri twice. You refuse to."

She'd never been a liar, nor was she about to start now. Crossing her legs, she lifted a shoulder. "Your business is with my fiancé."

He sat back, a hard glitter in his eyes. "I've offended you."

"Not at all."

"My reputation offends you."

"Perhaps we should choose another subject of conversation."

"I'd rather finish this one."

Oh, but he was a piece of work. There was no escaping

this. She set her gaze on his. "I don't like your business practices, Mr. Smirnov. But what I have to say is irrelevant to my fiancé's business."

He took a sip of his wine. "You think my association with Aristos will tarnish your family's reputation."

"I didn't say that."

He pressed the rim of his glass to his chin, his eyes on her. "The press like to print a lot of garbage about me, Aleksandra. Don't believe everything you read."

His smug they'll-never-catch-me look was too much for her. "Where there is smoke," she said softly, "there is usually fire, Mr. Smirnov."

Aristos returned from the cellar to find that Alex and Dimitri had moved to the lounge. Alex's stiff body language immediately had his antennae up. She excused herself not long after that, Galina at her side, happy to leave the business to the men.

Intent on solving his impasse with the Russian tonight, Aristos poured a liberal amount of brandy into their glasses. He wasted no time in getting to the point. "I need a firm commitment you're in, Dimitri."

The Russian lifted a shoulder. "I'm finding I need a faster return on investment these days. Your casino could be delayed for months. Years."

Aristos's blood pressure rose. "It won't be. Reports say Idas is ill. His son will come to the throne any day and it will be over."

"And if it isn't?"

His gaze narrowed. "Either you're in or you're out."

Dimitri sat back in the sofa, taking his tumbler with him. "I don't think your fiancée likes me."

"I'm sure you're mistaken."

"She doesn't like my business practices. She thinks

I'll be a detriment to your reputation. The royal family's reputation."

His back stiffened. "Did she say that?"

"That she doesn't like my business practices? Yes."

Alex had not said that. She would know better than to say that. Aristos's fingers tightened around the glass. "What the royal family thinks or feels is of no bearing to my business."

Dimitri inclined his head. "Still," he drawled, "I think the gestation time on this investment is going to be too long, I'm afraid. I'm out."

With those two words, the Russian put his casino on borrowed time. "I think you shoulder reconsider," he said tightly. "The prestige of this project will be like no other."

"Funny thing about that, Nicolades. It always seems that way until the next best thing comes along."

Aristos sat on the terrace by himself, putting away another glass of the brandy as he worked to control his fury... contemplated his future. He thought he had his temper under control by the time he let himself into the room where Alex was up, reading, but just looking at her made his vision go red.

She put the book down. "What happened?"

He threw his phone on the table. "He backed out."

"Why?"

"He said the gestation time of his investment was too long given the political situation in Akathinia."

"But that might change soon."

"He doesn't care."

"He won't change his mind?"

"No." He pinned his gaze on her. "Did you say you didn't like his business practices?"

A flush stained her cheeks. "He backed me into a corner, Aristos. You saw the games he was playing tonight."

"Which is why you should have said nothing." His voice rose. "Did you also tell him his business dealings with me reflected badly on the royal family?"

"No. He intimated that. I told him your business dealings were your affair."

"After you told him you didn't approve of his business practices!" He was yelling now and he didn't care. "How could you be so stupid?"

Her face lost all its color. She sat there for a moment, silent, then pushed the sheets aside, got out of bed and walked over to him. "You need to calm down. They'll hear you. I didn't say that. He did."

"After you said it at dinner the other night. Don't tell me it wasn't in your head."

"Yes, because I care about you. Because I don't think he's the type of man you should be doing business with. Because I worry about him being your downfall, not because it has anything to do with my family."

"If you cared about me, you would have said nothing." He threw his hands up. "All I asked you to do was entertain him, Alex, but you spent the night being the ice queen."

Her eyes widened. "Is that what I'm supposed to do? Keep my mouth shut? Perhaps I was not enough of a *political asset* to you tonight, then?"

He blinked. "What?"

"A political asset. Like you said to your lawyer on the phone today."

"You were eavesdropping on my conversation?"

"I came to ask about the wine."

"It was a throwaway comment." He turned and paced to the other side of the room, his head too full, too hazy with the alcohol he'd consumed to think clearly.

Alex watched him quietly. "I understand you are upset. I understand how important this night was for you. But this has been coming with Dimitri. You knew he was iffy.

So perhaps it was meant to be. You are meant to find a better fit."

Blood swirled in his head, making him feel as if it would blow off. He swung to face her, giving her a scathing look. "Oh, that's right. I'll just go round up another hundred-million-dollar investor. Give me a sec."

She bit her lip. "Do you know he employs underage girls in his clubs? Lord knows what they do beyond serving customers."

"Now you're letting your imagination go wild."

"And you're not seeing what's right in front of you. Or do you just not *want* to see it?"

"Alex," he growled. "I've never pretended to be a Boy Scout. I told you my world is full of gray areas."

"But *you* aren't." She shook her head. "You forget I know you now. You are a good man, Aristos, an honorable one. But if you don't watch it, this obsession with proving yourself *is* going to make you spiritually bankrupt."

His mouth twisted. "That happened a long time ago."

"No," she said. "It didn't. You did what you had to do to survive in the world. But now you have choices. Power. You need to decide which road to take."

Silence reigned between them. Lifting a shoulder, he went to the sideboard and poured himself a glass of water. When he turned around Alex was gathering up her things.

"What are you doing?"

"Going to my room. I think we could both do with some space."

"Running away, Princess?"

"No," she said, lifting her chin. "Walking away is your specialty. I'm calling a time-out."

CHAPTER FOURTEEN

ALEX'S TIME-OUT WITH Aristos lasted for two days. She was too angry with him for insinuating she was responsible for Dimitri's desertion to offer an olive branch, Aristos too busy working day and night to replace the Russian's investment to do so, either, apparently. Which had left them in a standoff that couldn't go on.

He had shut her out completely, rebuffed any attempt to talk as he made phone call after phone call to his contacts around the world. If she didn't break the impasse, she was worried he would build his walls back up completely before they worked this out, and she was far too invested in him for that.

She ate dinner alone for a second day, then decided enough was enough. Picking up the sandwich she'd asked the chef to make, she headed for Aristos's office. She found him standing at the window, hands braced on the sill, gaze trained on the remnants of the spectacular sunset.

She stood there for a moment, struck by what a solitary figure he cut. It clung to him like a second skin, as though he'd been wearing it so long it was his permanent finish. *The lone wolf.*

Her heart throbbed in her chest. For a while she thought she'd stripped it away, but now it was back.

She cleared her throat. "Any luck today?"

He turned to face her, his dark, fathomless gaze taking her in. "No. A couple of potential leads, but nothing substantial."

She put the sandwich on the desk. "You need to eat if you're going to function."

He didn't even glance at it. She leaned against the desk. "Are there other solutions to the loss of Dimitri? Can you scale the project back?"

An emotion she couldn't read flickered in his gaze. "I would have to withdraw the plans, make major adjustments, something I don't want to do when I've been so public about my vision for it."

His reputation would suffer. He would lose face. His big gamble to prove he had conquered the casino world a failure... "You would still be first," she pointed out. "The first to build a casino on Akathinia. Isn't that enough?"

His lashes lowered, framing the dark circles that rimmed his eyes. It would never be enough. He would constantly be chasing after the next big thing until he destroyed himself. The realization sent a chill through her.

"The industry is about vision," he said finally. "About convincing the entertainment world you have the biggest and the brightest offering. You lose that cachet and you're done."

"Or you lose everything because you need to save face. You don't need to prove yourself anymore, Aristos. You have achieved a success beyond most men's wildest imaginations. Perhaps part of a dream is better than none."

"I will find another investor," he rasped.

"Or you will destroy yourself trying."

He lifted his chin, his gaze a smoky, dark cauldron of antagonism. "Is your lecture almost done?"

"Not quite." She folded her arms across her chest. "You're still angry with me about Dimitri."

He shook his head. "You were right. He was already lost."

And he hadn't bothered to convey that to her? To apologize? A wave of antipathy washed through her. "You can be a real *jerk*, you know that?"

He lifted a shoulder. "I come as advertised."

Wow. She shook her head. "You're shutting me out."

"I'm working, not shutting you out."

"Funny, it feels as if you are. If you weren't, you would have apologized. We'd be talking, working through this together like a normal couple. Maybe I can't solve it for you, but I can be here for you."

"I told you I don't do this well."

"Oh, that's right, your convenient no-promises excuse, yours to pull out of the bag whenever you don't feel like communicating. You'd rather tune me out than be in a real relationship."

His gaze narrowed. "My company is on the brink. Cut me some slack."

"You did it before the poker game, too. This is your routine, Aristos. Your MO." She shook her head. "I want to be that person you can trust. I want to be the other half of *us*. But if you can't let me in, this is never going to work."

A dark glitter entered his eyes. "Maybe it isn't. I've been clear about who I am, Alex, and you refuse to see it. You keep pushing your sanitized Hollywood version of me."

Her chin lifted. "It's not a Hollywood version. It's you."

"It's not." He clenched his hands by his sides. "You want to know who I am? Who I really am? I'm the man who can't stick. Ever. I'm the man who walked out on his family not once, but twice, because he couldn't stick. The one whose father told him his family was better off without him. And guess what? He was right."

"No." She shook her head, heart clenching. "No, he wasn't."

"Yes." His olive skin was ashen, drained of color. "When my mother kicked my father out, my older brother, Vasili, came to me and asked me to come home, *pleaded* with me to help because he couldn't handle all the responsibility he'd been given, and what did I do? I said no. I told him my mother had already made her decision. That I was done with them."

Her heart fractured, a million tiny shards scattering in every direction, piercing her with their jagged edges. "You were hurt. You expected your parents to put you first."

"I was a piece of dirt, that's what I was. A street kid who didn't care, and I haven't much changed." He wiped a hand across his mouth. "So do yourself a favor and walk in the opposite direction."

"Aristos—" She put out a hand to touch him, but he shrugged it off.

"I have a call coming."

In other words, leave.

"Kala." She held his gaze, its bleakness chilling her. "But you're wrong. You are wrong about who you are. You're trying to give yourself adult decision-making skills when you were a child. You were acting on emotion, hurt, and the people who loved you should have known better. Done better."

Turning on her heel, she left before he broke her heart.

Aristos did the conference call with California, with little hope that lead would go anywhere. Everything he could accomplish done, every avenue exhausted, he sat back in his chair and closed his eyes. He'd slept maybe six hours over the past forty-eight, his body felt as if it had lead weights attached to it, yet still he sat there, racking his brain for alternate possibilities.

There were none. If his Los Angeles–based investor didn't bite, he was done. He would need to scale the casino back or pull the project entirely. Either way, his reputation would be in tatters, everything he'd built subject to the whims of an industry that would call you old news before the year was out.

He wanted to believe everything Alex had said, to absolve himself of the responsibilities he'd had toward his family, but the guilt went too deep. At sixteen, he'd been old enough to know what he was doing when Vasili had come to him, and still he'd made the wrong choice, a choice he knew would haunt him forever.

He rubbed his burning eyes, attempted to think past the haze consuming his brain. He knew he should go apologize to Alex, but he was afraid of what he'd say in this state of mind…afraid of saying things he'd regret.

Being around her made it impossible not to look at himself, at what he'd become, because she was the good, the lightness in this world. She made him feel better than he'd ever felt in his life, so close to that magical happiness quotient he thought it might actually be attainable. But the more he allowed his need for her to rule, the more vulnerable he became; the more out of control he felt.

She had the power to hurt him. To twist his brain into so many directions he didn't know what he wanted anymore. Who he was. And that terrified him, took him back to a place and time where that was all he'd felt, to a chaos he never wanted to experience again. Had sworn he never would.

He stumbled to bed at midnight, his head no clearer. Sure he would pass out, he lay staring at the wall instead. When he could resist no longer, he got up, went to Alex's room, scooped her into his arms and carried her back to his suite.

She looked disoriented, confused, her big blue eyes searching for his as he tucked her into his bed. He couldn't have her there without touching her. Sliding his hands over her curves, he rediscovered her, memorized her. With a low moan, Alex sank into his touch.

Exhausted and sated, he fell asleep with her in his arms.

Alex woke by herself after a night wrapped in Aristos's arms, a night in which everything had felt right again and she'd thought she might have gotten through to him.

When dinner passed and he was still holed up in his office, she told herself she couldn't expect massive change overnight. She slept in his suite that night, hoping he would come to her when he was done. She was asleep before he came in, and he was gone before she woke the next morning. The pattern went on for two days before the ache in her stomach began to make her feel physically ill.

A phone call from Nik interrupted her ruminations. Kostas had taken over in Carnelia and declared peace with the region. It was over. They were free to come home.

She was deluged with a mix of feelings—happiness she could finally return home, anxiety about what this would mean for her and Aristos.

When he deigned to make an appearance at dinner that night, she told him of her conversation with Nik.

He nodded. "He called me earlier this afternoon. I've asked the pilot to be ready to take us at noon tomorrow."

Just like that. Her fingers tightened around her wineglass. "What are we going to do?"

He gave her a quizzical look. "We fly home. Resume our lives."

Her heart, breaking piece by piece this week, fell apart a little further. "No," she said deliberately, "I mean what are we going to do about us?"

He frowned. "I need to get the financing for the casino sorted out."

"I think you need to get *us* sorted out while you're at it." She pushed her glass away. "You have to decide whether you're going to give me a meaningful place in your life or let me go, Aristos. It's as simple as that."

"It's not as simple as that," he growled.

"It is. I don't want to be a convenient wife, nor do I want to be a politically advantageous one. I want to be your partner. I want to be the one you come to when you're happy or sad. The one who licks your wounds for you."

The silence that followed was deafening. Hot tears pooled at the backs of her eyes. "Do you know the tabloids are making bets about how long we last? How long you can stay married?"

His eyes flashed. "They are garbage."

"Yes, but the funny thing about them is there's always a vein of truth there. It's how they survive."

She threw her napkin on the table and rose. "Tonight it's me who doesn't seem to have an appetite. If you'll excuse me."

Alex stepped into the helicopter behind Aristos the next morning with nothing between them resolved. She steadfastly refused to look down as they took off, bound for Akathinia. At all the memories the island held for her... the terrace where Aristos had held her through that wicked storm...the beach where he'd finally opened up and broken her heart...the beautiful, magical suite where she'd given him all of her, sure they were different.

She had no idea if they'd ever be back here together. If they'd even make it.

The journey was painfully silent, Aristos with his face in his laptop, her staring out the window. When the white Maltese stone Akathinian palace came into view, she knew what she had to do. She didn't want to live with a husband who cared about her the way her father had her mother, only commanding a piece of his heart; she wanted, needed, all of him.

The helicopter touched down. Aristos planned to continue on to his home on the outskirts of the city, then to his office, so the pilot kept the helicopter idling as her fiancé helped her out and onto the cement landing pad.

Stella and Nik appeared on the steps. Desperate to keep her emotions in check, she turned to Aristos. His expression was hidden by dark sunglasses, but what did it matter? He'd been emotionally unavailable all week.

He lifted a hand to run a finger down her cheek. "I'll call you later."

"Don't."

His head snapped back. She bit her lip, summoning a composure she wasn't sure she had. "We need some space, Aristos. Time to figure out how we feel about this. *Us.*"

"Alex—"

She put a finger to his lips. "I know how I feel about you. You know I love you. Now you have to figure out how you feel."

She kissed him. A brief touch of her lips to his. When he would have pulled her closer, she stepped out of his arms, turned and walked away, fighting back the tears that blinded her path.

He had taught her to grab hold of her future. Now she had. She wondered where it would take them.

Aristos stepped onto the helicopter after Alex threw those three loaded words at him and flew home. He spent the next week working the same insane hours, rattling around his too-big estate on the cliffs of Akathinia when he finally came home, its soaring ceilings and twenty-five rooms empty and without soul. They always had been, but it struck him now how utterly barren the place was.

He knew the difference was Alex, the effervescent presence she was, the spirit in her that reached out and surrounded him, refused to allow him to retreat into himself. But she had just walked out of his life.

It had been on the tip of his tongue to call her back, to rectify the mistake he knew he was making. But he'd known he wasn't ready. He had ghosts to exorcise, a future to shape. Wanting something, even as badly as he wanted Alex, wasn't proving you could stick. And that he had to do.

When word came that his final hope for an investor to replace Dimitri had fallen through, it was like being handed a life sentence he'd known was coming. All you could do was slide your hands into the shackles and admit your mistakes. Your failings.

Alex had been right. He would destroy himself trying to prove something that didn't matter anymore. He needed to stop. He needed to find a peace he could live with.

A lightbulb went off a few nights later, pulling him out of bed and to a sketch pad, where he drew until morning. He sent the amateurish result to his genius of an architect, asking him what he could do to modify the current casino design with that direction to save costs but still retain his vision. Then he waited. And waited. When Barry Schindler flew in two days later, arriving on Aristos's doorstep to find him unshaven and ready to pounce, he gave his client a wry look.

"Losing some sleep?"

"Just a bit."

"I might be able to help."

Two strong espressos sitting on the table beside them, the architect took Aristos through the redesigned plans. His design was inspired, based on lighter, more versatile materials and brilliant, indiscernible modifications that would provide no less of an impact.

"How much?" Aristos asked, chest tight.

"I've saved you fifty million."

Which left him fifty million short. Perhaps he could get his other investors to kick in the remainder… It was worth a shot.

He made his first phone call to his biggest investor at a US bank. He said yes. He made more calls. A funny thing happened then. As word spread that Dimitri was out, his investors started calling *him* to offer to make up the gap. They'd never liked the Russian's involvement.

By the end of the week he had his fifty million and a go-ahead from the Akathinian government to break ground. A front-page story ran in the business section of the newspaper with the new schematic included. It was garnering universal acclaim.

The story also included a feature on the program he had committed his company to—what he called the Hector Rigatos Gambling Addiction Fund. He wouldn't call it that, of course, but he would forever think of it as that. For what Alex had taught him.

An intense feeling of satisfaction, of rightness, settling through him, he set the newspaper down, walked out onto the balcony and took in the hauntingly beautiful view of the mountains. In the shadow of that quiet, majestic presence he knew it was time for him to take *his* leap. He couldn't right the wrongs he'd made with his family— they would forever be with him—but he *could* change the future. If he wanted to be with Alex, to deserve her, he needed to face his demons. He needed to go home. He needed to learn how to stick.

CHAPTER FIFTEEN

SMILING AND WAVING at crowds during Akathinia's annual Independence Day celebration, even one as joyous as it was this year with the prospect of war lifted from the national conscience, was no fun for a princess who'd rather be on an Aegean island with the man she loved.

Alex was navigating her new role with care, loving her work with Nina, settling back into palace life with its intricacies and formalities. If only she didn't feel so miserable. If only she could put last week's newspaper feature out of her head.

Aristos had secured his investment, the casino was a go, the ground-breaking to happen in two weeks' time. But what had made her put the paper down and leave the breakfast room in tears was the gambling addiction fund he'd created to help those who fell through the cracks.

She was so happy for him. And still he hadn't come.

Her heart throbbed painfully in her chest as they navigated the final length of the parade route on the float upon which she and her family stood. Perhaps she'd been wrong. Perhaps it was just too difficult for Aristos to let down his walls after decades of shoring them up.

Somehow, she managed to hold her smile as they reached the end of the parade route, bade the crowds goodbye and were ushered into the waiting limo. Only her father was missing, his recovery at home an unexpected development as his archnemesis, Idas, lay on his deathbed.

Her father hadn't seemed to warm up much to her, but

her budding relationships with her siblings gave her such joy. Stella, who was becoming the best friend she'd always wanted in a sister. Nik, whose quiet, wise philosophy held so much she could learn from.

Stella pounced as the limo came to a halt in front of the palace and Alex slid out, heading for the stairs.

"You have to stop moping around."

Alex swept up the stairs and through the doors. "Aristos isn't coming tonight He's playing poker on Vardis Melonakos's yacht."

"You told him you needed space."

"That was a cue for him to give his head a shake."

"Maybe you should give yours one, too."

She pulled to a halt. *"Really?"*

"Yes, really. He's crazy about you, Alex. I saw it on his face when you walked away from him at the helicopter… when he pursued you at the press conference."

Her mouth pursed. "I'm not sure he's emotionally capable of acting on it."

Stella followed her up the stairs and into her bedroom. "Perhaps not, but moping around on the biggest day of the year isn't going to help. Are we going to have fun tonight or are you going to act like a limp dishrag?"

She straightened her shoulders. Gave her head the shake she knew it needed. "Yes," she said firmly, "we are going to have fun."

She channeled her favorite literary heroine for inspiration. *What would Scarlett do?*

She would *not* sit around pining for Aristos while he played poker on Vardis Melonakos's yacht with beautiful women serving him drinks. She would show him what he was missing.

"I think we should go shopping."

"Shopping?" Stella looked at her as if she were mad.

"My legs are about to fall off. The ball starts in four hours."

"Do you want to help me or not?"

The two princesses entered the Akathinian royal ballroom arm in arm after a firestorm of paparazzi flashes documented their arrival.

"A prior engagement," Alex had said tersely when asked where her fiancé was.

Stella shoved a glass of champagne into her hand. "Drink."

She did. Her sister scanned the room, her gaze settling on Crown Prince Kostas of Carnelia, standing beside Nik in a group near them.

"Look at him walking around the place as if he owns it. I *hate* him. I don't care what Nik says, what they said in their little *chat* together, there is nothing on this planet that could make me like him."

Alex smiled. Prince Kostas's unexpected appearance at the Independence Day ball had been a shock to everyone. Nik had invited the prince as a symbol of the healing that needed to happen between the two countries. Stella, still brokenhearted over her eldest brother's death at what she called "Kostas's hands," had not taken it well.

"Perhaps you should listen to what Nik has to say," Alex suggested. "He seems to be at peace with it all."

Stella scowled. "Kostas is a coward. He spent the last year relegating our two countries to turmoil, afraid to stand up to his father. I have no respect for him."

As if the extraordinarily handsome crown prince's ears were burning, he turned his head toward them. Elegant in a black tuxedo, he wore his dark hair short and cropped above a face that could be described as nothing short of spectacular: high, aristocratic cheekbones; piercing, narrow eyes beneath thick dark brows; and a straight, prominent nose.

"He's awfully stunning, Stella."

"If arrogant brutes are your idea of attractive, yes."

"I thought you used to like him. They say he is progressive, pro-democracy, nothing like his father. Apparently very witty and intelligent."

"*Used to* being the operative words."

Alex's eyes widened as Kostas broke away from the group and headed toward them.

"Don't look now, but here he comes."

Hot color stained her sister's cheeks. "Here? Why is he coming over here?"

"We're about to find out."

The crown prince stopped in front of them and inclined his head in a greeting. Alex smiled politely, but Kostas's gaze had moved to Stella and stayed there. "Perhaps you would do me the honor of a dance?"

A loaded silence followed. The flush in her sister's face deepened, her lips pursing as if to refuse. But then her manners seemed to kick in, as if she knew they were being watched, and with a stiff nod, she accepted.

Which left Alex alone. Alone in the very sexy dress she'd purchased, the plunging neckline of the champagne-colored sequined gown skirting the limits of what a princess might get away with. Worn perhaps to show the world she didn't care her fiancé wasn't here—or perhaps the man himself.

She stood, back against a pillar, watching Stella and the prince dance. It was better than TV. Two men asked her to dance, the duke Aristos had liked to make fun of and a friend of Stella's, but she turned them both down, pleading sore feet, a poor excuse, but she didn't care. She was tired of pretending.

"I was standing over there wondering why the most

beautiful woman in the room keeps turning down dances," a deep male voice purred in her ear. "Instead of allowing my imagination to run wild, I thought I'd come over and find out for myself."

Aristos.

Her heart jumped into her mouth as she turned to face him. He was not in a tuxedo like the other men, but in a dark suit that made him look so handsome her heart stayed lodged right where it was, deep in her throat, making speech nigh impossible.

The tears she'd been fighting swamped the backs of her eyes, threatening a full release.

"Oh, no." Aristos's gaze darkened. "No tears, Princess, not when we've come this far."

She swallowed hard, fighting them back. *What did that mean?*

"Aren't you supposed to be playing poker?"

"I was. I found my attention was elsewhere, so I left."

She scowled at him. "I am not available as a *diversion.*"

"Funny," he drawled, his gaze sliding over her. "That dress screams it with a capital *D*. It's not fit for public consumption."

"Absentee fiancés don't get a say in the matter."

Fire lit his gaze. "Ah, but we know they do. Especially since I am not absentee any longer."

He curled his fingers around her forearm and directed her out of the ballroom to the terrace. Bypassing the crowd there, he led her down into the gardens. They walked until they came to the fountain, the little square at the center of the maze where he'd challenged her to take her big jump.

She sat down on the lip of the fountain, the sounds of the party muted now, the square deserted.

Aristos sat down beside her, splaying his long legs in front of him. The scent of his spicy aftershave made her want to crawl into his arms. She wrapped hers around herself.

"You asked me for space," he said, setting his dark, inscrutable gaze on her. "And you were right—I needed it. Needed to figure myself out, determine my priorities, whether I could be the man you needed."

Her heart squeezed. He always had been.

"What I discovered is that my life as I've been leading it is not the life I want to live. You made me see that, angel, made me see the possibilities…what I want, and I want more. I want to wake up every morning with you beside me. I want to share my life with you. I want you to be there to lick my wounds when I stumble, and yes," he added a devilish glitter in his eyes, "other parts of me, too."

Her heart turned over, leaping with a joy that sent it tumbling nearly out of her chest. "Aristos—"

He held up a hand. "I have a lot of baggage, Alex. Maybe more than I can ever fully overcome. There's never going to be a day where I'm not cognizant of the fragility of life—of how everything can be taken away from you in the blink of an eye. It will always make me a fighter. It will always push my survivor instincts to the forefront, making my first inclination to push people away. It's a reflexive thing I'm going to have to work on."

A tear slid down her cheek. "All of us have those things…those crutches we rely on. For me it was retreating. Not taking the chances I should. You showed me that."

"For me it was burying the past. Trying to pretend it never existed, that it couldn't hurt me, but it was always there in the background, chasing me. I knew after you walked away from me I would regret it if I let you go. But I had to face my ghosts first. Find out who I am now. Who I *was*. So I went home."

Her heart leaped. "You did? How was it?"

"Painful. Awkward. Amazing."

She could so identify. And yet hadn't it all been worth it?

"I'm so glad you went," she said softly. "Were they glad to see you?"

"Yes." The rasp in his voice made her cover his hand with hers. "I think there is…potential there. My mother—she was very emotional. Vasili—he—he will be the hardest. I broke his trust. I need to get it back."

She crawled onto his lap then, because she couldn't resist. Her hands framed his face. "You've made the overture. Give it time."

He nodded, his eyes so full of emotion her tears became a steady flow, sliding down her cheeks and soaking his shirt. She kissed him, a long, sweet kiss full of salty tears and the future she knew they had in front of them.

He pulled back, his hands grasping hers and dragging them to her sides. His gaze was so serious, so full of intent, it made her stomach grow tight. "You saved my soul, angel. I was very nearly spiritually bankrupt. I need you with me to make sure that never happens again, that my demons don't take over."

She gave him a tremulous smile. "I think I already made that commitment."

He lifted her ring-clad finger to his mouth and brushed his lips over her knuckles. "I think I missed something when I gave this to you."

"What?"

"I love you, *agapi mou*. I think it was love at first sight, if the truth be known. I did everything but say no to Nik when he asked me to take you to Larikos."

He loved her. Her brain latched on to those three words and held them tight. "I told him it wasn't a good idea," she breathed. "I knew you were trouble, Aristos Nicolades."

"I am," he murmured and proceeded to demonstrate with a kiss that had no sweetness to it, only hunger, an insatiable hunger that seemed to have no end. She moved closer as he slid a hand to her bottom and brought her to him, his sexy, fiery kisses leaving her short of breath.

"Your bedroom," he murmured as they came up for air, "where is it?"

Procuring a bottle of champagne along the way, they climbed the stairs to the royal suites. She was in his arms kissing him before they made it halfway up, then again outside her bedroom door before he pushed it open and shoved her inside.

She pouted as he lost his jacket. "I thought it was spiritual for us."

"Yes, angel, it is." He started working on the buttons of his shirt. "Now I'd like to take it to another realm."

She took a drink from the bottle. Eyed him. "I love you, Aristos."

His gaze darkened as he looked up at her. "I love you, too, Princess. Now put down the bottle and get over here."

She did. Because sometimes dreams *were* too expensive to keep. And sometimes they were all that mattered.

* * * * *

Look out for the dramatic conclusion of
KINGDOMS & CROWNS
Coming soon!

And you can find out where it all started in
CARRYING THE KING'S PRIDE
Available now!

#3437 WEDDED, BEDDED, BETRAYED
Wedlocked!
by Michelle Smart
When Elena Ricci is kidnapped by Gabriele Mantegna, she never expects her body to ignite with Gabriele's every touch! As the chemistry that blazes as brightly as their hatred builds, will it lead to a legacy that will last a lifetime?

#3438 EXPECTING A ROYAL SCANDAL
Wedlocked!
by Caitlin Crews
For Felipe Cairo to avoid the shackles of duty, he must choose a *most* inappropriate wife, and Brittany Hollis has an unrivaled reputation. Until a twist shocks them *both*...Brittany might not be queen material, but she's carrying a royal heir!

#3439 SIGNED OVER TO SANTINO
by Maya Blake
Three years after sharing one night of oblivion with Javier Santino, Carla Nardozzi needs his help! The Spanish aristocrat seizes his chance for revenge on the only woman to walk away from *him*— Carla must become his lover!

#3440 THE SURPRISE CONTI CHILD
The Legendary Conti Brothers
by Tara Pammi
After nearly losing her life, Alexis Sharpe determines to tell Leandro Conti about their child. Leandro regrets how he treated Alexis seven years ago, but now that she's back and the mother of his child, he will claim *everything* that's his!

YOU CAN FIND MORE INFORMATION ON UPCOMING HARLEQUIN® TITLES, FREE EXCERPTS AND MORE AT WWW.HARLEQUIN.COM.

HPCNM0516RB

"Mistress," Nikolai slotted in, cool as ice.

Shock had welded Ella's tongue to the roof of her mouth because he was sexually propositioning her and nothing could have prepared her for that. She wasn't drop-dead gorgeous…*he* was! Male heads didn't swivel when Ella walked down the street because she had neither the length of leg nor the curves usually deemed necessary to attract such attention. Why on earth could he be making *her* such an offer?

"But we don't even know each other," she said dazedly. "You're a stranger…"

"If you live with me I won't be a stranger for long," Nikolai pointed out with monumental calm.

And the very sound of that inhuman calm and cool forced her to flip around and settle distraught eyes on his lean, darkly handsome face.

"You can't be serious about this!"

"I assure you that I am deadly serious. Move in and I'll forget your family's debts."

"But it's a *crazy* idea!" she gasped.

"It's not crazy to me," Nikolai asserted. "When I want anything, I go after it hard and fast."

Her lashes dipped. Did he want her like that? Enough to track her down, buy up her father's debts, and try to buy rights to her and her body along with those debts? The very idea of that made her dizzy and plunged her brain into even greater turmoil. "It's immoral… It's blackmail."

"It's definitely *not* blackmail. I'm giving you the benefit of a choice you didn't have before I came through that door," Nikolai Drakos fielded with glittering cool. "That choice is yours to make."

"Like hell it is!" Ella fired back. "It's a complete cheat of a supposed offer!"

Nikolai sent her a gleaming sideways glance. "No, the real cheat was you kissing me the way you did last year and then saying no and acting as if I had grossly insulted you," he murmured with lethal quietness.

"You *did* insult me!" Ella flung back, her cheeks hot as fire while she wondered if her refusal that night had started off this whole chain reaction. What else could possibly be driving him?

Nikolai straightened lazily as he opened the door. "If you take offence that easily, maybe it's just as well that the answer is no."

Don't miss
BOUGHT FOR THE GREEK'S REVENGE
by Lynne Graham,
available June 2016 wherever
Harlequin Presents® books and ebooks are sold.

www.Harlequin.com

HPEXP0516